TRULY
TAN

TRULY TAN

BY JEN STORER

Illustrated by
CLAIRE ROBERTSON

ABC
Books

For Miss Bell, who said my handwriting was very good indeed. – JS

To Amelia and Lily, my daily sources of joy and inspiration. – CR

The ABC 'Wave' device is a trademark of the
Australian Broadcasting Corporation and is used
under licence by HarperCollins*Publishers* Australia.

First published in Australia in 2008
as *Tan Callahan's Secret Spy Files*
by Penguin Group (Australia)
This edition first published in 2012
by HarperCollins*Publishers* Australia Pty Limited
ABN 36 009 913 517
harpercollins.com.au

Text copyright © Jen Storer 2012
Illustrations copyright © Claire Robertson 2012

The rights of Jen Storer and Claire Robertson to be identified as the
author and illustrator of this work have been asserted by them in
accordance with the *Copyright Amendment (Moral Rights) Act 2000*.

HarperCollins*Publishers*
Level 13, 201 Elizabeth Street, Sydney NSW 2000, Australia
31 View Road, Glenfield, Auckland 0627, New Zealand

National Library of Australia Cataloguing-in-Publication entry:

Storer, Jen, 1961–
    Truly Tan / Jen Storer ; illustrated by Claire Robertson.
    ISBN: 978 0 7333 3121 3 (pbk.)
    For primary school age.
    Detective and mystery stories–Juvenile fiction.
    Robertson, Claire.
A823.4

Cover and internal design by Stephanie Spartels, Studio Spartels
Cover illustrations by Claire Robertson
Image on page 92 © Samum/Dreamstime.com
Images on pages 26, 51, 57, 90, 126 and 190 by iStockphoto.com
Printed and bound in Australia by Griffin Press
The papers used by HarperCollins in the manufacture of this book are a natural,
recyclable product made from wood grown in sustainable plantation forests.
The fibre source and manufacturing processes meet recognised international
environmental standards, and carry certification.

5 4 3 2   12 13 14 15

Contents

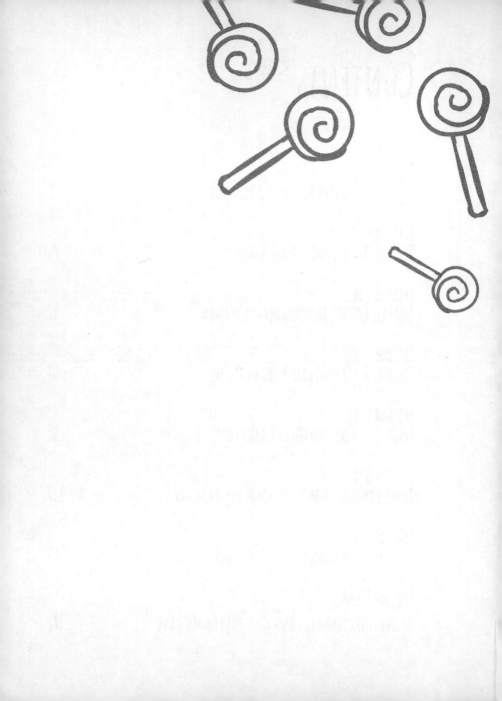

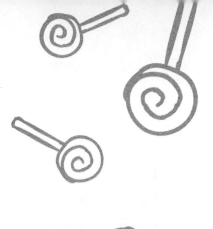

Episode One:

Lollipops, Ginger Beer and a Dead Fox

1

My mum lives in la la land. This is what she called my big sisters: Emerald, Amber and Rose. It makes them sound like traffic lights – or lollipops. When I was born, Mum said Dad could do the naming. But it still had to be a colour. So Dad chose Tan. I like it.

Right now I'm looking through my telescope. My eye has landed on two men in a dusty truck. I don't like the look of them. They look shifty and I would know. I have the mind of a Great Detective.

'Tan! You better have that telescope packed. The truck is here!'

That's Miss Bossy Britches, Emerald. We're moving house today. Not only that – we're moving to the country. This is a serious thing. This is a big mistake. I truly think that.

I put my telescope in a box. 'See you at the other end, old friend,' I say.

'Tan? Come along! And don't forget a squirter bottle for the animals. It's your job to keep them cool.'

'Coming, Mum,' I say. I pull out my binoculars, hang them around my neck and head downstairs.

We follow the removal truck in our van. Our van is jammed with people and stuff. Mum and Dad are in the front, with bags and pillows and things they forgot to pack. Then come the lollipops, with bags and pillows and things they forgot to pack. Doodad's in there somewhere, too. Doodad is Amber's dog. She's a poodle chihuahua cross. Amber says she's a 'choodle'. I say she's a '*poo*huahua' (with the emphasis on the *poo*).

POOHUAHUA: say, *poo-wah-wah*. The poohuahua is an annoying little dog. It looks like a fluffy slipper. It smells like a fluffy slipper. But do not be fooled. The poohuahua is nowhere near as smart as a fluffy slipper.

Finally there's me, with my binoculars, my notebook, my squirter bottle and Awesome. Awesome is my dog. He's huge. He's awesome. He's always depressed.

In the very, very back there are some other members of our family – the ones who travel in cages. There's Queen Victoria (we call her QV for short). She's a tortoise. She's fond of travelling. There's E, but no one can see him. He's right at the back of his cage, seething. And there's Babbles.

Babbles is clinging to her perch, like one of those wooden birds that are carved out of wood. She keeps going off like a microwave,

Ding! Ding! Ding!

She always does the microwave thing when she's tense.

We drive for ages, past houses and buildings and thousands of signs. Past parks and high-rises and hospitals. Through tunnels and over huge bridges where you have to pay. Finally the city is just a smudge in the sky behind us. The lollipops groan.

'We'll be *so* out of range in this horrible place,' says

Emerald, poking at her old mobile phone.

'And what about my dancing?' says Amber. 'Country people don't do ballet. Everyone knows that. I'll be the only dancer in the village. I'll grow old and crazy and people will see me dancing with a broomstick at midnight. They'll say, *"There goes Amber Callahan, the lone dancer. Poor thing. She never had an audience."'*

'You're nuts, Amber,' says Emerald. 'Anyway, we don't have *villages* in this country. That's just real estate talk.'

Rose sits there combing her doll's hair and muttering to herself. Yes, Rose still plays with dolls. Although her dolls are *strange and unusual*. A bit like Rose, really.

'What about you, Tan?' calls Dad from the front. 'Want to add to the complaints?'

The lollipops spin around and look at me.

'Well,' I say slowly, 'apart from the fact that I will be fifty thousand miles away from Molly and I'll miss our old place and I'll have to go to a new school and I'll be stuck out in the middle of nowhere, I guess I'll be fine ... Oh, yes, and I'll have to set up a new World Headquarters. I don't know who I'm going to spy on, though. Maybe the cows ...'

'Oh, dear,' sighs Mum. 'Cows are such dull creatures.

I hope we don't have too many dealings with—'

'Well, would you look at that,' Dad interrupts. 'The removal truck just took the wrong exit.'

'Maybe they know a short cut,' I say, watching the truck through my binoculars.

'Well, if they get there before us, I hope they find a shady spot to wait. They haven't got a key to the house,' says Dad. 'I wouldn't give them one. They looked shifty to me.'

Mum rolls her eyes, but I just smile to myself. I knew it!

We drive and drive and drive. It's hot and it's sweaty. Awesome wears his special cap. The one with the battery-operated fan.

'No wonder that dog's depressed,' says Emerald, fanning herself with a *Cosmo* magazine. 'I'd be suicidal if someone made me wear a hat like that.'

'But Awesome loves this hat!' I say. 'The fan keeps his face cool.'

Awesome stares at the floor.

By lunchtime, Babbles is making internet noises, so we know she's feeling better. QV is enjoying the sights. Her head is bobbing like one of those toy dogs you see in the back of old people's cars. But E is still nowhere to be seen. He's got a wet towel over his cage to keep him cool. It's doing nothing to cool his temper.

At last we pull over. Dad parks the van under a giant peppercorn tree and Mum pulls out an Esky, a picnic basket, rugs, pillows, hats, a CD player, glasses, a coffee plunger, a beach umbrella, a vase and a bunch of flowers.

'Good enough to photograph, darling,' says Dad.

Mum looks pleased. Mum writes for fancy food magazines. You know, the ones for people who eat things like 'gorgonzola' and 'field mushrooms'. Every meal in our place is a major production, even a picnic on the side of the road – in 35-degree heat.

```
GORGONZOLA: the most disgusting cheese
known to man. Do not attempt to eat it.
Do not even attempt to sniff it.

FIELD MUSHROOMS: mushrooms found in
a paddock. Known to grow in and around
cow poo. Personally, I would not eat them.
```

Awesome flops under a tree and a fly settles on his nose. His hat has a flat battery. I suspect that's why he's so gloomy. I go and sit by him. It's weird how you always want to sit down after you've been sitting down for ages. Sitting down is an exhausting thing to do.

Doodad leaps out of the van. She's not tired. She's puffing and panting and dancing about on her back legs. She's wearing doggy sunglasses and a hairclip with a seahorse on it. She looks ridiculous.

'That dog will have a heart attack one day,' I say. 'It is a very uptight animal.'

'She's just excited, aren't you, Doody?' says Amber. Doodad spins around and snaps at the air.

'Well, I'll have a heart attack if she keeps doing that,' says Mum.

'Dance, Doodad,' says Amber firmly, and Doodad sits. Doodad has a scrambled brain. She was the runt of her litter. Her owners didn't want her. That's why Dad brought her home to us. He felt sorry for her. All our animals are ex-patients of Dad's.

Dad puts E's cage under a tree. We can see his eyes gleaming at the back of the cage, but he still refuses to budge.

'He'll settle down once we get there,' says Dad cheerfully.

There's a quiet growl from inside the cage.

Emerald puts Babbles under another tree. A tree that is a long way from E.

'Choose a cushion,' calls Mum. 'Lunch is ready. And, Tan, keep Queen Victoria away from the centrepiece. I don't want her eating my daisies.'

We all gather around the edges of the blanket. There's a china bowl full of chicken pieces, another bowl of homemade potato salad, crusty bread rolls and a jug of Mum's homemade ginger beer – with ice shaped like stars in it.

There's also some rocket lettuce and a marigold for QV.

MARIGOLDS: cruddy little orange flowers that nobody really likes (except maybe tortoises). Often known as *'stinkin' Rogers'*. (I have no idea who Roger is. I expect he smells like a marigold.)

'Delicious, darling,' says Dad as he heaps up his plate for a second helping.

'Hey, don't take all the wings!' says Emerald as Amber goes in for another grab.

'Manners, please,' says Mum, lifting QV away from the centrepiece. 'We might be entering the wild, but we are not *going* wild.'

Babbles starts ringing like our old doorbell. It reminds us all of home. Everybody sighs. Dad tells Babbles to shush.

After lunch, Mum pulls out a toffee apple for each of us: green for Emerald, orange for Amber, red for Rose and brownish, tannish, murkyish for me.

'Right,' says Dad, 'round up the troops. If we leave now, we'll be there by dark.'

It's hard to believe we're actually getting somewhere. We pile back into the van and head off. I lean against Awesome. I have my toffee apple in one hand and my binoculars in the other. I do regular checks of the scenery. But there's not much to report on. Just trees, rocks and the occasional cow. Mum's right. Cows are dull.

Finally, just as it's getting dark, we leave the highway and start driving down this really skinny road that has lots of trees and bushes on both sides. Dad pulls a crumpled piece of paper from his pocket. He hands it to Mum.

'Okay,' he says. 'From now on it gets complicated. You'll have to read me the directions, Coral.'

'**Deeper and deeper,**' says Rose, in a creepy voice. '**Deeper and deeper the city family drove into the evil forest.**'

'Stop it, Rose!' says Amber. 'You're creeping me out!'

'**Deeper and deeper,**' says Rose, waving her fingers in Amber's face. 'Don't look back, Amber Callahan. Don't look back. Oh, no! Someone's tapping on the roof!'

Amber whacks Rose on the arm. 'Mum, make her stop!'

Rose sits there with a weird smile on her face. Her braces glint in the moonlight. It makes her look … unpredictable.

'Stop it, Rose, you're scaring your sister,' says Mum. Then she looks at the piece of paper and squints. 'Lou, it says here we have to turn at the *dead fox*. Is that some sort of quaint little country pub?'

'No,' says Dad. 'It actually is a dead fox. The real estate agent hung it over a fence post to mark the turn.'

'Ha!' says Rose. 'Beware the dead fox. They say the eyes follow you ...'

Amber squeals and flicks Rose with a magazine. Emerald wriggles down in her seat and turns up her MP3 player. I peer through my binoculars, but it's too dark. All I can see is blackness that stretches forever, and looming trees that crowd the sides of the road and glow like silver ghosts in the headlights. I put my arm around Awesome. He yawns.

In the back, Babbles is making microwave noises and QV has disappeared into her shell. There's a low rumble from E's cage.

'There it is!' cries Emerald suddenly. 'The dead fox!'

2

Dad slows down and the headlights fall on the dead fox.

'It's watching us!' says Rose. 'It moved!'

Amber screams and throws a blanket over her head.

'How nasty,' says Mum as Dad swings the van onto a dirt road. 'A dangling carcass is hardly a warm welcome.'

'Yeah, well,' says Dad, craning forward to watch the road, 'the real estate agent was a funny sort. Big guy. Had a blue sports car with "I'd rather be hunting" on the bumper. Barry Crisp, I think his name was.'

'Well, Mr Crisp certainly has a sick sense of humour,' says Mum. 'We'll get rid of that fox as soon as we settle in. It's appalling.'

The road is rough and dusty and it twists and turns. The lollipops start to whine again. Even Rose. I start to worry, too. It is my serious hope that Dad knows the way out.

Suddenly there are headlights coming toward us.

'Well, I'll be,' says Dad. 'You don't expect to see anyone out here ...'

He pulls the van over to make room for the car ahead. As it gets closer, we can tell it's going fast. Dust is foofing all around it. *Vrooom!* It zooms past us, honking its horn. It's a removal truck. It's OUR removal truck and it's going the wrong way! The shifty men wave and hoot as they fly by.

'That was our truck,' says Dad.

'That was our furniture,' says Mum.

'That was my life!' says Emerald.

I enter the truck's number plate into my notebook. I knew those guys were shifty.

We drive on for a little while and no one says a thing. The van rattles and bumps and Doodad gives an occasional whimper.

'It's no use chasing them,' says Dad finally. 'We'll track them down tomorrow.'

'Maybe they unpacked for us,' says Mum hopefully.

'But they didn't have a key,' says Dad. 'No, I'd say they were lost. Probably been going round in circles. Probably didn't even know it was us back there.'

'Hmm,' says Mum. 'Are there any nice hotels close by?'

'None that take two dogs, an angry cat, a bird and a tortoise,' says Dad.

Mum sighs. We all sigh. So this is our new life. Driving around in the middle of nowhere with an empty house waiting for us, and everything we own, including my precious telescope, gone forever.

'I'm going to totally *die* without my hair straightener,' says Emerald. 'And my magazine collection and—'

'What about my dance costumes?' says Amber. 'And my tiara collection? This is the end of my career. *The end of the magnificent Amber Callahan.*'

'My dolls,' says Rose, and she tucks her knees under her chin and starts rocking backward and forward. 'My dolls. My sketches. My dolls. My sketches …'

'Don't be such a bunch of pessimists,' says Dad. 'We'll get our stuff back. You'll see.'

Dad looks over at Mum, but Mum just stares straight ahead. I suspect she is thinking about her brand-new, **stainless steel, state-of-the-art** mix-mash-and-whiz master.

Not long after, Dad turns the van into a long, gravel drive. It has trees all the way along it.

'Here we are,' he says. 'We're home.'

We all sit up and try to see our new house. All we can see is a giant hedge. We drive through the hedge. The house is big. It's white. It has a veranda that goes all the way around. And I think it's got an attic! But there's something strange about it. In the dark, our new house looks kind of like a junkyard.

Dad pulls up. We scramble out and then it hits us – everything we own is on the front lawn. The fridge, the washing machine, the dishwasher, the TV, the couches. Boxes and boxes of stuff. The shifty men in the dusty truck have dumped everything on the front lawn. And left.

'Told you we'd get our stuff back,' says Dad.

It's dark. We're tired, we're starving and we just want to get inside.

'You unlock, love, and I'll bring some of these boxes in,' says Dad to Mum.

'I thought you had the keys,' says Mum.

'No,' says Dad. 'I gave them to you.'

'But I thought—'

It goes on and on like this, until finally Mum and Dad admit that neither of them have the keys.

Emerald loses the plot. 'See! I knew we should never have come to this place. I tried to tell you but would anyone listen?'

'**'Tis the fox,**' says Rose, her eyes shining. '**'Tis the curse of the dead fox. They say it haunts the—**'

'Muuum!' says Amber. 'Rose is doing it again!'

'Oh, be quiet, all of you,' says Mum. 'Your father and I need to think.'

We watch silently as QV shuffles over to the veranda steps.

She stretches out her head and sniffs.

'We could sleep up there,' I say quietly.

'What?' says Mum.

'We could camp on the veranda,' I say. 'Our mattresses are already up there.'

Everyone looks. Our mattresses are in a wobbly stack on the veranda.

'Yeah, right,' says Emerald. 'Good one, Tan.'

'Yeah,' says Amber, 'if you think I'm gonna sleep out here, you've got another think coming.'

'No, hang on,' says Dad. 'It's not a bad idea. We could sleep under the stars tonight, then tomorrow I'll go into town and find a locksmith.'

'But what about the mosquitoes?' says Mum.

'And the spiders?' says Emerald.

'And the wild animals?' says Amber.

'And the curse?' says Rose.

What a bunch of pessimists! I leave them to whine and take off. I check every single box till I find the ones marked camping. I tear them open.

'It's all here!' I yell. 'Sleeping bags, candles, matches. There's even a torch.'

I flick the torch on Awesome. He blinks in the spotlight. 'See!' I say. 'Even Awesome thinks it's a good idea.'

By the time everyone has agreed on where they want their mattresses, and Emerald has found her magazines, and Amber is wearing her favourite tiara, and Rose is drawing a dead fox in her sketchbook, and Mum has checked her brand-new, stainless steel, state-of-the-art mix-mash-and-whiz master, and Dad has fed the animals, and we've eaten the leftover chicken and drunk the flat ginger beer, Mum and Dad are too tired to stop us playing murder in the dark. Emerald says she's too old for murder in the dark, but she plays anyway, just to make sure we don't get freaked.

It is a scary thing to play murder in the dark when you don't know your way around, and your front yard looks like a junkyard, and there are creepy trees and a thick hedge that people like Rose can jump out of at any time. In the end, Amber gets really freaked, and Mum yells, and that's when we stop playing.

The lollipops crash on their mattresses. I get out my telescope and set it up. But there's no one to spy on.

No neighbours. No cars. No buses. No suspicious pedestrians looking suspicious. **Nothing suspicious at all.** But there are stars. And there is a moon. And I think, but I am not sure, that I can see Mars. It is the first time I have seen such a thing.

Dear Diary

I am writing to you by the light of my tropical
island mosquito candle — you know, the one that
smells like fly spray. Everyone else is asleep, except for
Amber. She keeps opening one eye. Rose told her, 'the
dead fox walks at night'.

I have never slept on a mattress in a sleeping bag on a
veranda in the country. When we live here properly,
I am going to do it again. Maybe even often.

Tomorrow morning I have to remember: I bags the attic.
It will make the perfect World Headquarters.

I think I saw a tree house. But maybe I didn't.

I am thinking that moving here may not have been a mistake. But I am not sure of this thought.

Today I learned this: it is boring to be a pessimist.

Truly
Tan

P.S. The country has a very big sky.

Episode Two:

Secrets, Skulls and Purple Haunt

Snap. Click. Crunch. Rose is loading up her box brownie. A box brownie is a camera. It is a very old camera. It is so old it doesn't even have batteries. It is hard to think how it ·must work.

'Where are you going with that box brownie?' I ask.

'I'm going to photograph the dead fox,' says Rose.

Hmm. This sounds like an interesting idea.

'Sounds like an interesting idea,' I say, and I run to get my bike.

When I get back, Emerald and Amber are standing with Rose.

'Where are you going with that box brownie?' says Emerald.

'I'm going to photograph the dead fox,' says Rose.

'Hmm,' says Emerald, and she runs to get her bike.

Amber just stands there with her mouth open. Then she says, 'You're all mad. You'll catch the curse; you know that, don't you?'

'This box brownie can photograph curses,' says Rose. 'It will show the dead fox. And it will also show the curse hanging over it.'

Amber's eyes nearly pop out of her head.

We all ride off.

'Wait for me!' yells Amber.

It is a long, dusty ride to the fence post where the dead fox hangs. It's hot, too, but Awesome doesn't notice. He just stares at his feet as he lopes along beside us. Doodad rides in Amber's basket. Doodad is smiling. She is a very stupid dog.

She doesn't know she is wearing a bow with sequins on it. If she did, she would be embarrassed.

> **SEQUINS:** sequins are little sparkly things. Amber's dance costumes have sequins. Mum's old evening dresses have sequins. Things with sequins belong on people, not dogs. You cannot respect a dog wearing sequins.

Rose has a map so we can find our way down the twisty road to the dead fox fence post. We have only been living here in the country for one night. Today we are investigating.

'This is it,' says Rose finally.

We look around. There's a fence post. But there's no dead fox.

'It's gone,' says Emerald.

'*Wicked!*' says Rose, jumping off her bike. 'The dead fox lives!' She takes some photos of the bare fence post.

'Oooh,' groans Amber, 'I feel like one of those tomb raider people. We'll all be cursed. The dead fox will come back and—'

'Don't be an idiot,' says Emerald. 'It's *dead*. And we're not tomb raiders. We're just four sisters stuck in this stupid, boring wilderness.'

There's a noise in the bushes.

'Something's there,' I whisper.

Amber jumps and Doodad yips.

'On guard,' I whisper to Awesome. Awesome sits and scratches his ear. He is not a very dedicated guard dog.

We are just about to ride off, when the bushes part.

A boy steps out.

'Thought I heard something,' says the boy.

The boy has a hessian bag in his hand. I do not like the look of the hessian bag. It is a **highly suspicious** hessian bag.

'Who're youse?' says the boy.

'Who are *you?*' says Emerald.

'I'm Ted,' says the boy. 'This is our land.'

'What's in that hessian bag?' I ask Ted.

'What's it to you?' says Ted.

At this point, I decide that Ted is a very rude boy. But I continue my investigations. 'That bag looks suspicious,' I say. 'We would like to know what's in it.'

'Wow!' says Ted, looking at Awesome. 'That dog is awesome!'

'How do you know that?' I ask.

'Know what?' says Ted.

'My dog's name,' I say.

'What?' says Ted.

'Oh, never mind!' says Emerald. 'Are you going to show us what's in the bag or not?'

'Can't,' says Ted.

'Why not?' says Emerald.

'Cos you're girls and girls *blab*,' says Ted.

Emerald puts her hands on her hips. I can tell she's about to say something ... hostile.

HOSTILE: this is a word our family often uses to describe Emerald. When Emerald gets hostile, we mostly stay out of her way. When I am a teenager, I wonder if I will get hostile.

I don't want Emerald
to scare Ted off.
It is suddenly very
important that we find out
what's in the hessian bag. I put
my hand on Emerald's arm. 'I'll
handle this,' I say quietly.

Emerald looks at me. Or maybe
she glares at me. Anyway, I take over
the investigation.

'Ted,' I say, 'if you show us what's in that
bag, we'll let you see our photos of the curse.'

'What?' says Ted.

'Rose here has a special camera,' I say. 'This camera
takes photographs of curses. There is a big curse floating
about this fence post.'

Ted looks at the fence post. Then he looks at the
box brownie. I can tell he's never seen anything like it.
He looks at Rose. I can tell he's never seen anything like her.

'Weeeell,' says Ted, thinking it over.

'I'll let you play with Awesome,' I say quickly. (Ted doesn't
know that Awesome NEVER plays.)

'All right,' says Ted, 'but first you have to stand in a circle of truth and promise not to blab.'

'Oh, for goodness sake,' says Emerald. 'You are such a little—'

'Sure, Ted,' I say, fast. 'Draw a circle of truth and we'll stand in it. Won't we, Emerald? Won't we, Rose? Won't we, *Amber*?'

Amber is clutching Doodad to her chest. Amber is worried about what might be in the hessian bag.

Ted grabs a stick and draws a big circle in the dirt. We all step into it.

'Now, promise not to blab,' says Ted. 'No matter what you see here today.'

'We promise,' I say, and I frown at my sisters.

'We promise,' they mumble.

'Good,' says Ted. He kneels in the circle of truth and opens the hessian bag. Slowly, he tips it upside down. We all take a step back …

First a hammer slides out, then a box of nails, a paint brush, a box of Smarties, a butter knife and finally … a skull!

Amber screams and leaps out of the circle of truth. She grabs her bike. 'He's crazy!' she yells, stuffing Doodad in her basket. 'A lunatic! What kind of kid carries a human skull?'

Rose pokes the skull with her toe.

'Careful!' says Ted.

Rose picks up the skull and holds it in the air. 'It's a sheep's skull,' she says, waving the skull around.

Ted grins. 'Excellent, isn't it?' he says. 'Not a mark on it.'

Ted turns to Amber. She looks like a piece of petrified wood that is so petrified it can't move.

'Are you from the city?' he says to Amber. But Amber doesn't answer.

'We're all from the city,' says Emerald. 'Only, some of us are dumber than others.'

```
SKULLS: in case you don't know, here is
something to remember about skulls: you
will never, ever see a human skull with a
snout. I know this because my dad is a vet
and he has vet books with lots of pictures.
Animal skulls have snouts ... or beaks.
Human skulls do not have snouts or beaks.
```

Ted starts putting the stuff back in the bag.

'Ted,' I say, 'why do we have to keep this stuff a secret? Why did we have to go in a circle of truth for a silly old sheep's skull and a hammer?'

Ted looks at me. 'It's not the stuff that's a secret,' he says. 'It's what I'm using it for that's a secret.'

'Yeah, right,' says Emerald. 'So, are you going to tell us what you're using it for?'

'I'm not gonna tell you,' says Ted, standing up. 'But I am gonna show you. You'll have to leave the bikes, though. Bikes can't go where we're going. It's a jungle. No human has ever set foot there … except for the Chosen Few.'

'Cool,' says Rose.

Even Emerald looks interested. Amber is still staring at the hessian bag.

We leave our bikes by the cursed fence post and follow Ted, single file, into the bush.

'What if he turns on us?' whispers Amber. 'He's got a knife!'

'He's puny,' I whisper back. 'I could flatten him with one karate kick. Or Emerald could give him a slap. Besides, we've got Awesome.'

At this point, Awesome pushes past me to the front of the line.

'Hey there, boy,' says Ted. 'Come to say hello, have you?'

Awesome licks Ted on the hand. *He licks Ted on the hand.* I can't believe it! Awesome never licks anyone on the hand. Not even me and I am his faithful owner!

I stop and look at Ted patting Awesome, and Awesome smiling up at Ted, and suddenly I feel ... hostile.

'Hurry up!' calls Rose, over her shoulder. 'We're losing him!'

We all yell at Ted to slow down and we stumble after him. I do not like this Ted boy. He is rude and hostile-making. But I keep following him, because I must know his secret. I am very interested in other people's secrets.

Eventually there comes a time when we have been pushing our way through the bush for too long, and Emerald is thinking that Ted tells lies, and Amber is saying that Ted is a criminal, and Rose is wondering if Ted is deluded. I am not sure what deluded means, but Rose says Amber is deluded, so I'm thinking it is not a good thing to be deluded. Anyway, just as we are thinking all these bad things about Ted, we stop. We can hear water. Not only that. We can hear music. Irritating music. It is from the musical called *Cats*. Mum and Dad took us to see *Cats*. It was a silly show. The actors did not look like cats at all. They looked like actors with too much fur and make-up. But Mum and Dad didn't care. They loved *Cats*. They played the music for months. This is why I know the music from *Cats*. This is why I hate the music from *Cats*.

'Here we are,' says Ted, and he holds the bushes apart so that we can step out into a clearing.

We stand with our mouths wide open. It is an **amazing thing** that we see before our eyes. If this amazing thing were mine, I would definitely keep it a secret.

4

Before our eyes is a cubby house. But this is not the kind
of cubby house I have grown used to in my life. This cubby
is nearly as big as a real house. It stands high on stilts, with
stairs going up. The cubby is painted dark, dark purple
with white around the windows. It has many sorts of skulls
nailed to the walls. It has a veranda. There is a girl on
the veranda. She is listening to *Cats* music
and doing ballet steps. She is
wearing silly frilly leggings,
and has a tiara like Amber's
on her head. The cubby
house has a letterbox. And
over the letterbox hangs ...
the dead fox.

'*Sweet!*' says Rose, and she
starts to take photos of the
dead fox and the purple
cubby with the skulls.

Amber looks at the dancing girl on the veranda. Then she looks at the skulls and the dead fox. It is my thought that Amber is confused. Amber does not know whether to clap for joy or turn hysterical and scream.

HYSTERICAL: people who are hysterical usually start screaming. They say things that don't make sense. Hysterical people are out of control. It would be just like Amber to turn hysterical.

The girl on the veranda stops dancing and looks down at us.

'Ted!' says the girl. 'Who are these urchins you have brought before me? They are NOT of the Chosen Few.'

'Are you a dancer?' says Amber, staring up at the girl. 'I'm a dancer. I come from the city, and I have twelve tiaras, and costumes with sequins, and this is my dog, Doodad. You can hold her if you like ...'

'Ted,' says the girl again. 'Bring me the one they call Doodad. Now!'

'Put a sock in it, Jem,' says Ted.

We are all staring at Jem on the veranda. But Ted isn't. I think Ted thinks Jem is ... deluded.

'Welcome to Purple Haunt,' says Ted as he drops the hessian bag on the ground. 'It's the biggest secret. If you tell anyone, you'll end up like the dead fox.'

'Whatever,' says Emerald.

Now I know Emerald is impressed. I think I might be impressed, too.

But just then, we hear a big splash.

There's a creek running by Purple Haunt and that's why we could hear water when we were back in the bush.

I swing around. It's Awesome! He has fallen in the creek!

'Awesome!' I scream, and I run down to the edge of the water.

By now, Awesome is out in the middle. I can't see his legs or his tail or his body. All I can see is his big sinking head, which is gasping for air. Awesome has never been in a creek or a river or even a toddler's toddling pool. Awesome won't even play under the hose.

'He's drowning,' I yell. 'We must save him! Call an ambulance! Call Police Rescue! Call the fire brigade!'

I start pulling off my runners and emptying my pockets.

'Don't be a dork,' says Ted. 'He's havin' a swim.'

'What would *you* know?' I say to Ted. 'Awesome is my dog and he has never been swimming in his life. He hates water. I know because he's MY dog.'

'You're hysterical,' says Ted, and he throws a stick at Awesome.

'What are you doing?' I scream. 'Do you want to sink him?'

'Calm down, Tan,' says Emerald. 'Ted's right. Awesome's having a ball.'

I can't believe Emerald is siding with Ted. Emerald is *my* sister. Awesome is *my* dog. I am thinking there are traitors among us. I am thinking I don't like living in the country one little bit. It is a bad luck place.

But then I notice something. Awesome has the stick in his mouth, and he is not sinking. He is moving closer to us.

'Wow,' says Rose, and she takes a photo. 'Awesome's an excellent swimmer.'

Awesome hauls himself out of the creek. He drops the stick at Ted's feet. Then Awesome shakes like a shaking machine and every one of us gets soaking, dripping wet (except for Amber and Jem. They are up in Purple Haunt trying Jem's tiara on Doodad).

When Awesome finally stops chasing sticks, and swimming in the creek, and shaking water over us, we decide we are hungry. Ted says he has Smarties in his hessian bag, which of course I remember, because I have the mind of a Great Detective. I do not miss any details.

Ted says he will share his Smarties with us. There are six of us and twenty-seven Smarties, so Ted says it's easiest if the girls get three each and he eats the rest. Either Ted can't count or he thinks we're dumb.

Three Smarties are not very filling. So then Jem makes a plate of fairy bread because Ted has a butter knife in his hessian bag and now she can spread butter. Jem says, 'Share with us this humble offering and by these means you shall become at one with the Chosen Few.'

Ted rolls his eyes and says it is hard work having such a strange sister. This is the first sensible thing he has said all morning.

Amber practically swallows her fairy bread whole. She is desperate to become one of Jem's Chosen Few. Emerald complains that all this sugar is bad for her skin and Rose gets hundreds and thousands stuck in her braces. But it is nice fairy bread all the same.

After that, we say goodbye to the dead fox and Purple Haunt, and Ted reminds us that we better show him the box brownie photos as soon as they get developed or we will be kicked out of the Chosen Few. Then Jem says that Ted is a rude host, but he leads us back to our bikes anyway. We are in a hurry because we have to get home and help Mum and Dad unpack. Also, we know Mum will have cooked something delicious by now. But we don't tell Ted that.

'Emerald,' I say as we are riding home, 'what was that little building out the back of Purple Haunt?'

Emerald looks at me and laughs.

'It's a drop dunny,' honks Rose, pinching her nose.

'A drop dunny?' I say. I still don't know what they're talking about.

'Yeah,' says Emerald 'It's one of those toilets that don't flush. It's really just a big hole in the ground.'

'With a wooden seat over it,' adds Rose. 'They stink to high heaven.'

'Yuk!' says Amber. 'That's disgusting. I'd rather wee behind a tree.'

It is the first time I have ever agreed with Amber.

Dear Diary

I am writing to you by the light of my woody brown camouflage flashlight — you know, the one that looks like an innocent stick. I like my new bedroom, but it is not an attic. When I said, 'I bags the attic,' Mum just pushed past me with her cookbooks and her laptop and said, 'The attic will make a glorious office.'

I got hostile today and I am not even a teenager. Amber nearly got hysterical, so that's worse. Awesome nearly drowned. But then he learned to swim.

I have a code for Purple Haunt because Purple Haunt is the biggest secret. My code for Purple Haunt is PH. I think I will like PH very much. But probably not Ted.

Rose said she will develop her box brownie photos in the laundry. She said it will be a 'covert operation'.

I said she should keep it a secret.

It is a surprising thing to live in the country.

I wonder about the dead fox.

Truly
Tan

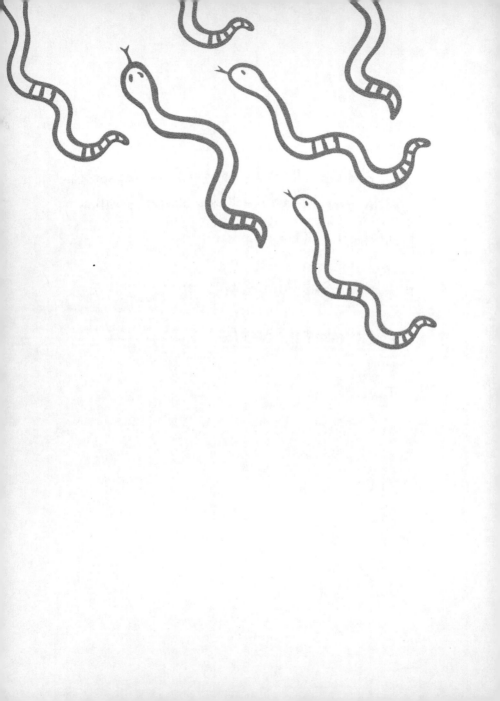

Episode Three:

Snakes, Ghosts and Wandering Wanda

5

Ted has a dead snake in a jar. It is on a shelf in Purple Haunt. Ted says it is a very rare snake. He says if you get bitten by one of these snakes, your eyes will roll back in your head and your brains will boil in your skull and you will be fairly dead, fairly quickly. Ted says the snake in the jar is called a black-eyed brain-boiler. I am highly suspicious of this. I am highly suspicious of anything Ted says.

I asked Mum what she knows about black-eyed brain-boilers. She said she knows nothing, but they sound alarming. I will ask Dad what he knows about black-eyed brain-boilers. Meantime, I am thankful they are very rare snakes.

I would like a snake in a jar for World Headquarters. I have been setting up World Headquarters all morning and it's looking good. I saw the tree house on our first night here. We were playing murder in the dark at the time and I was in a hurry. I wasn't sure if it was a tree house. But it is and I bagsed it, so now the tree house is mine – even though it has bits of wood hanging off it. And a few holes in the floor. And Mum said it was disgusting because it was full of possum poo and bird nests.

Anyway, I scrubbed it and Dad did some hammering and now I think World Headquarters is exactly like Purple Haunt. Except not everyone can stand up straight in World Headquarters. And it doesn't have a veranda. Or a door. Or real windows. Or a creek. Other than that, World Headquarters is exactly the same as Purple Haunt, and Ted would definitely be jealous if I ever invited him over. Which I won't.

This is what I have in World Headquarters: my telescope, my binoculars, my Spy 'n' Pry magnifying glass that is not a toy, my Secret Spy Files (which detail everything suspicious I have ever observed), a world globe, and a corkboard with a photo of my best friend, Molly (who is manning our city branch of World Headquarters). I also have a red beanbag, a chair, a desk, a pencil tin, a walkie-talkie and a waterproof torch. There is also my cicada collection, an emu egg, a jar of fool's gold that I am sure will be valuable one day, a poster of a meerkat eating a giant scorpion, my Magic 8 Ball and my box of disguises (including the vampire teeth I wear some nights to turn Amber hysterical).

E is up here, too. I don't know why. E has his own chair on the veranda, but he prefers World Headquarters. He sleeps on a cushion in the darkest corner. He hisses occasionally. I do not attempt to talk to him. I do not attempt to look at him. E prefers it that way. He is a very angry cat. As for Awesome, he can't get into World Headquarters. Awesome can't climb ladders and I can't lift him, so he is stuck on the ground.

Woof! Woof! That's the doorbell I have wired up for World Headquarters. The button is at the base of the ladder and when you push it, the doorbell barks like a dog. It must have been invented by a genius.

'You rang?' I say, hanging out the window.

Amber is at the base of the tree. 'Emerald and Rose say the coast is clear,' she whispers. 'Meet us in the laundry in *five* minutes. If you're late, you'll be locked out!' She runs off.

I am excited to hear that the coast is clear. We have been waiting for this chance for two days. We have been waiting for the coast to be clear so we can develop Rose's secret box brownie photos.

Before I go to the laundry, I consult the Magic 8 Ball. 'Magic 8 Ball,' I say, 'will Rose's box brownie photos reveal the curse that is hanging over the dead fox?'

I close my eyes and give the Magic 8 Ball a shake. I check the answer. It says, **DON'T COUNT ON IT.**

I have never had much faith in the Magic 8 Ball. Especially since Amber dropped it on the concrete. I toss it on the beanbag, slip my vampire teeth in my pocket and hurry down the ladder. I don't want to be locked out of the laundry. I don't want to miss seeing the curse.

The laundry in our new house isn't like it was in the city. This laundry is outside the house, off the back veranda. It's big and old and there is heaps of room for a darkroom.

DARKROOM: a darkroom is ... a dark room. You develop photos in a darkroom. Not even a crack of light is allowed in, or the photos will disappear and all you will have left is a wet piece of paper. You use a special, spooky red light in a darkroom so you can see a little bit and you don't spill the photo chemicals and slip and whack your head and get tangled up and wreck the photos etc.

Rose has already blacked out the laundry window and hung a sign on the door. It says, DARKROOM IN USE. ENTER ON PAIN OF DEATH.

I knock gently. I truly hope I am not too late.

'Took your time,' says Emerald as she opens the door.

'Four minutes, twenty-one seconds to be precise,' I say.

'Well, come in before Mum hears,' says Emerald, tugging my arm.

Of course, I know for certain Mum won't be hearing us.

She's up in the attic writing an important article for *Dainty Palate*. The article is called 'Coming to terms with your scones'.

'Is Dad around?' I ask as I enter the darkroom.

'He's in town,' says Rose, and she flicks off the light.

Suddenly the laundry is a very dark room. In fact, it is pitch black. For a moment there is silence. Then Amber whispers, 'What now?'

We don't usually go in dark darkrooms with Rose. It is a foolish thing to do. Besides, Rose's photos are usually weird and boring. But this time she has photos of the *paranormal*. This is the only reason we would enter a darkroom with Rose.

PARANORMAL: ghosts and curses and spirits are part of the paranormal. It means these things are just not normal. Sometimes I wonder if Rose belongs to the paranormal. And maybe E, too.

'I can't see,' whines Amber. Amber is fidgeting. This means she's getting scared.

I don't know why, but it is a funny thing to see Amber scared.

Click!

Amber jumps and an eerie red glow lights up the darkroom.

'Let the magic begin,' says Rose, and she laughs a deep, **evil** laugh.

Amber grabs the door handle. 'Do that again and I'll open this door and your stupid photos will be ruined!' she says.

'Woah,' says Rose. 'I'm sooo scared.'

Rose looks spooky in this red glow and Amber looks spooked. I am thinking this would be an excellent time to pull out my vampire teeth.

'Come *on*,' says Emerald. '*Focus*. Or we'll never get out of here.'

Rose gets busy sloshing around with tubs of chemicals and photo paper and camera film. She is acting like she is all important and we are … not.

Actually, it is quite interesting to watch photos develop. It's a bit like magic. First there's nothing, then a picture starts to form and you see it unfold before your very eyes. If you have ever written a top-secret note using invisible ink, you will know what I am describing. Anyway, we all watch closely as, one by one, Rose pegs the dripping photos on the photo line and the secrets of the box brownie are revealed.

It is hard to make out all the details in the red light, but the first thing we see is a photo of the ground. Then one of Rose's fingers, the wheel of someone's bike, and an intriguing close-up of Doodad's ear. Then there is a terrible photo of Awesome drowning. Then one of Awesome shaking water all over Ted. I like that one very much. Then there's the dead fox fence post.

We all squeeze in close and try to see the curse. But it is a disappointing photo. It has not captured anything that looks like a curse. It fact, the fence post does not look one bit paranormal. It's just standing there looking woody.

'Perhaps the Magic 8 Ball was right,' I say as I squint at the photos.

'What?' says Rose.

'Nothing,' I say.

The next photo is a close-up of the actual dead fox as it hangs over the letterbox at Purple Haunt. I notice that the fox has half its left ear missing, but apart from that it looks like a normal dead fox. Rose still swears that the fox is cursed, but the photo does not prove her theory. The photo is not sufficient evidence that there is anything at all paranormal anywhere near that dead fox. This is what I would call a disappointing outcome. I am cross because Ted will say, 'I told you so.'

'Can we open the door now?' says Amber.

'There's one more,' says Rose.

We all lean in as Rose pushes the last photo into the tub … It's Jem on the veranda of Purple Haunt. You can see the skulls that are nailed to the walls of PH and you can see Jem doing her ballet steps.

'Now *she* is definitely paranormal,' I say, and Rose and Emerald laugh.

'She's not paranormal!' says Amber. 'She's beautiful and talented and … misunderstood.'

'More like *mis*combobulated,' says Emerald, and Rose and I laugh again (even though we don't know what miscombobu-thingy means).

Rose pegs up the last photo and Amber moves in for a closer look. And that's when she screams, and Rose nearly whacks her head, and I nearly slip, and Emerald nearly gets tangled in the photo line.

'What's the matter with you?' yells Emerald. 'You scared us half to death!'

Amber has her hand over her mouth and she is pointing at the photo of Jem on the veranda. 'Isaghst!' she says through her fingers.

I will translate this for you. What Amber actually says is, 'It's a ghost!'

For a second no one says anything. Then I take control. 'This requires further investigation,' I say as I take down the last photo. 'I need to take this to World Headquarters.'

For once the lollipops agree with me and we leave the darkroom and hurry along the back veranda and up the ladder into World Headquarters. E growls as we enter, and his crooked tail swishes back and forth.

'Nice kitty,' says Amber, and E hisses. He does not enjoy being called 'kitty'.

I grab my Spy 'n' Pry magnifying glass and hold it over the mysterious photo. 'Remarkable,' I whisper, for this is the only word I can think of.

'Give me that,' says Emerald, and she snatches my Spy 'n' Pry magnifying glass.

'Careful!' I say. 'It's not a toy, you know.'

Emerald stares at the photo for the longest time and Rose gets impatient. Amber hangs back and bites her lip.

'Well?' says Amber finally. 'What is it?'

'It could be a face,' says Emerald.

'It's definitely a face,' says Rose darkly, and she holds the photo up to the light. 'It's a face from **the other side.** Look how it's hovering. It's a ghost for sure.'

'I knew it,' squeaks Amber, and she flops onto my beanbag.

Now, it's true that the box brownie photos are all in black and white and this makes them look a bit … unearthly. Even the photo of the ground looks shimmery. But there is no doubt that this last photo has a paranormal ghost in it. You can see the ghost almost very clearly. Its grey face is crinkly and it is hovering in the trees behind Purple Haunt. The face has wispy white hair floating around it that is definitely not leaves. The face is so ghosty that sometimes you can't even see it properly. But it's there.

'That ghost has its eye on Jem,' I say.

Amber groans.

'We must warn them,' says Rose. 'We must take this photo to Purple Haunt right now and warn Ted and Jem.'

'But we could never find Purple Haunt on our own,' says Amber. 'It's too hidden.'

'She's right,' says Emerald.

'Awesome will led us back to Purple Haunt,' says Rose. 'He loves Ted.'

'Well, I think it is ridiculous to say that Awesome *loves* Ted,' I say. 'That is an exaggeration. Awesome loves me because he's my dog and—'

'Oh, get over it,' says Emerald. 'Come on. Let's get out of this stinking tree house and see if your dopey dog can lead us back to Purple Haunt.'

'He's not dopey,' I whisper as I follow the lollipops down the ladder. 'And you're the stinky one.'

I'm not sure if I approve of the fact that Awesome leads us straight back to Purple Haunt. On one hand, it proves to my sisters that Awesome is not dopey. He is, in fact, a sophisticated hunting dog. On the other hand, it also proves that Awesome *might* like Ted. I know this because when we get there, Awesome and Ted act like long-lost friends. Which they are not.

'So you're back?' says Ted. He looks up at us as he rubs Awesome's ears.

'That is ObViOUS, Ted,' I say.

Jem is on the veranda of Purple Haunt. She waves a silk scarf and nods her head at Amber. 'You may come up if you wish,' she calls. 'The parlour is tidy. I am ready to receive guests.'

'Later,' calls Rose. 'You better come down here, Jem. We've got something to show you.'

We sit in the shade and Rose pulls the paranormal photo out of her bag.

'Cool,' says Ted. 'A photo of The Haunt.'

'Look more closely,' says Rose.

'What do you see in the background?' says Emerald.

'Concentrate,' I say.

Ted and Jem look closely. We all hold our breath …

'Trees?' says Ted.

'Open your eyes, Ted!' I say. 'Look harder.'

'What *is* this?' cries Jem suddenly. 'What is this ectoplasmic vision you have captured?'

We all stare at Jem.

'Ecto … what?' says Amber. 'What are you saying, Jem?'

'I'm saying, there is a ghost in those trees,' says Jem.

'**Yes!**' says Rose, and she gives me a high five.

ECTOPLASMIC: I don't know what
ectoplasmic means. It is surprising
to think that someone like Jem knows
such a big word. Perhaps she made it up.
Ec-to-plas-mic. I like this word.

Ted grabs the photo and takes another look.

'Oh, right,' he says. 'You mean those shadows? I s'pose they look a bit like a ghost. If you believe that sort of stuff.'

'A *bit*?' I say, taking back the photo. 'That's more than a bit of a ghost, Ted. That is a real, live ghost.'

'Looks more like Wandering Wanda to me,' says Ted, and he gets up and throws a stick to Awesome.

'It's not Wandering Wanda,' says Jem.

'Course it is,' says Ted.

'It can't possibly be,' says Jem quietly.

'Stop!' says Emerald. 'What are you talking about? Who's Wandering Wanda?'

'Wandering Wanda is this crazy old lady who lives in a shack at the back of our neighbour's farm,' says Ted. 'She's related to our aunty's grandfather's big sister. Or something weird like that. Anyway, she went nutty.'

Awesome drops the stick at Ted's feet and Ted picks it up.

'Wandering Wanda killed the black-eyed brain-boiler with her bare hands,' says Ted, twisting the stick as if he's wringing its neck. 'That snake's been in our family for years.'

'But that can't be Wanda in the photograph,' says Jem, and her voice is a bit wobbly.

'Why not?' says Emerald. 'She was probably spying on us. It makes sense.'

'It doesn't make sense at all,' says Jem.

'Why not?' says Rose.

'Because Wandering Wanda is *dead*!' cries Jem.

'What?' says Ted. 'What do you mean?'

'She dropped dead in front of Ye Olde Real Estate Agents two weeks ago,' says Jem, and Ted's jaw drops wide open.

Now, I have the mind of a Great Detective and this new information leads me to a new conclusion. If the ghost in the trees looks like Wandering Wanda, and Wandering Wanda dropped dead in front of Ye Olde Real Estate Agents two weeks ago, then the ghost in the trees must *be* Wandering Wanda. But I am left with one nagging doubt.

'If that ghost is Wandering Wanda,' I say, 'why would she haunt Purple Haunt? What's of interest to her here? Why wouldn't she haunt her old shack ... or Ye Olde Real Estate Agents? What are Wandering Wanda's motives?'

Ted looks at me and frowns.

'A ghost would not do any haunting without a serious motive, Ted,' I say. 'Even you must know that.'

'You,' he says, 'are seriously weird.'

Dear Diary

I am writing to you by the light of my plastic skull lamp — you know, the one with the green light bulb between its teeth.

I asked the Magic 8 Ball to solve the mystery of the tree ghost. 'Magic 8 Ball,' I said, 'was that really the ghost of Wandering Wanda in the trees behind Purple Haunt?' The Magic 8 Ball said,
YOU MAY RELY ON IT. I have always had great faith in the Magic 8 Ball. It is a valuable tool.

I looked up 'miscombobulated'. It is not a real word.

I looked up 'ectoplasmic'. It is something to do with ghosts.

I have added a new section to my Secret Spy Files. It is the `Paranormal Ectoplasmic` section. Wandering Wanda is in it.

Dad has not heard of black-eyed brain-boilers, but he has heard of yellow-bellied black snakes. I asked him if he would put one in a jar for me. He said it was highly unlikely.

I am thinking about my new school. I don't know how to be the new girl. I wish Molly was here. You really need a friend when you haven't got any friends.

Ted buried the dead fox.

Truly
Tan

Episode Four:

School, Skeletons and a Shaky Mouse

6

Dad gave me a cat skeleton. It is on a special stand on a shelf in World Headquarters. It is a real cat skeleton – the bones are made of real bone, not plastic bone like those trick skeletons. Dad used the cat skeleton when he was learning to be a vet.

When E saw my cat skeleton, his hair stood on end and his tail spun and he hissed and spat. The cat skeleton has big teeth and empty eyes and this is probably why it makes E jumpy. I unhooked one of the cat skeleton's front legs and put it in a drawer. Now the cat skeleton only has three legs, just like E. I hope this helps him relax.

Sometimes I would like to be E. Sometimes I would like to lie on a cushion in a dark corner in a world-class tree house and hiss. I would especially like to hiss about going to a new school. This is something very hissable.

'Tan! You better get down here now. We're leaving in five.'

Emerald is yelling as usual. She is excited because today she is starting year eight and Amber is starting year seven.

Emerald says it is very important to be in year eight and that Amber better do what she says, because she knows everything about high school and Amber doesn't.

'Don't forget to bring something special for your first Show and Tell, darling,' calls Mum. 'And hurry along.'

'Okay,' I mutter, looking around World Headquarters.

I consider bringing QV along. QV is a good talking piece. People like to look at her and talk. But really, she is just a tortoise – she's grey and slow and she can be a snob. She might insult someone. This is a risk I am not prepared to take. No, I need something fascinating for my first Show and Tell. Something *envy-making*. Something that will definitely make me the popular new girl from the city. My eyes land on the cat skeleton. Purrrfect.

I place the cat skeleton in its box and carefully slide it into my backpack. Then I grab the silk scarf from around my Magic 8 Ball. I have a brilliant Show and Tell plan.

In the country, there is a bus that takes us to school. In the city, Mum drove us. But our country schools are too far away. We have to take a bus.

There are already other kids on the bus when we get on. I have not been on a school bus before. It smells like … Vegemite and old socks. I don't look at the other kids as we walk down the aisle, but I know they are staring.

Emerald pretends she doesn't know us and sits down the back. Amber sits with Rose. That leaves me. I sit on my own and look out the window. I pretend there is something fascinating out the window. But mostly what I see is my own reflection.

I balance my backpack on my lap. It is my sincere hope that the cat skeleton travels well. The cat skeleton is my ticket to popularness.

POPULARNESS: I am not 100 per cent certain that popularness is a real word, but it should be. It is a useful word. I could say, 'my ticket to greatness'. But I want more than greatness. I want popularness.

Before long, the bus stops – and Ted and Jem get on. Amber climbs over the seats to get to Jem and they go off and sit together. I make room for Ted, because I think it might be interesting to talk to him about Purple Haunt and Wandering Wanda. Ted looks at me. Then he looks at Rose. Then Ted walks straight past us and plonks down next to a boy with sticking plaster on his nose. Ted doesn't even say hello! Ted is a bad-mannered country boy and this is another reason why I don't like Ted.

It is a long dusty drive to school and the bus gets noisier as we go. It gets crowded up, too. Someone sits next to Emerald. Someone sits next to Rose. But no one sits next to me. I am thinking this might be a good thing, but I am not sure why it might be good thing. Then, just as I'm thinking these complicated thoughts, a girl sits down next to me. She has crooked hair with a wonky fringe and a 'science week' tattoo on her forearm.

'I'm Lily,' says the girl. 'Do you like my tattoo? I got it in a show bag *three* weeks ago and it still hasn't washed off. Of course, I'm very careful when I wash my arm and I put plastic over it when I go swimming. If you look closely, you can see the edges are starting to fray.'

I look closely at Lily's tattoo. The edges are definitely starting to fray. But it is a good solid tattoo all the same.

'Impressive, isn't it?' says Lily.

I nod. 'You have interesting hair,' I say, and this is true.

'Thanks,' says Lily. 'Do you have something special in that backpack?'

'Secretly special,' I say.

'I can tell by the way you're holding it,' says Lily.

Lily is very observant. I think I am going to like her.

We drop off the high-school kids first. Amber links arms with Jem and they hurry off the bus, whispering. It is my guess they are whispering about something dumb. Emerald looks at me as she walks past my seat. I look at her, too.

'Who's that?' says Lily.

'That's Emerald,' I say.

Lily nods.

'She's in year eight,' I say.

Lily nods again.

'She's got a mobile phone.'

'Really?' says Lily. 'Does it work?'

'Sometimes,' I say.

When we get to our school, everyone piles off the bus in a big scramble. They go in all directions. There's not much organisation in this new school. A group of girls surround Lily and she disappears.

'The grade four classroom's over there,' says Rose. 'You go—'

'I know where to go, Rose,' I say. 'I was at orientation, too, you know. As if I'd forget my way around a little country primary school.'

'Suit yourself,' says Rose, and she runs off.

I look around. The little country primary school is much bigger than I remember. It wasn't this big when I came here with Dad for orientation. Perhaps they added more buildings over the holidays. I think they added more kids, too.

The cat skeleton is getting heavy and my stomach feels floaty. It is not a nice feeling. I take a seat at the edge of the basketball court. I wonder if new girls always have floaty stomachs.

'Tan Callahan, I believe?' says a voice behind me. 'Welcome to Peppercorn Grove. I trust you know your way to class?'

It's Mr Lamble, the deputy principal. Mr Lamble wears a dark grey suit and a green bow tie. He has tiny spectacles that are almost as small as his eyeballs. Mr Lamble is a very extinguished gentleman.

'Yes, thank you, Mr Lamble. I do know my way around,' I say politely.

'Very well then, Tan. No time to waste. Off you go.'

'Yes,' I say, hopping up. 'Off I go.'

This might be a strange thing for me to say, especially as I don't actually *go* anywhere.

Mr Lamble frowns. He takes off his eyeball spectacles and gives them a polish. I like his bow tie. I don't imagine it squirts water though ...

'Through those front doors and fourth on your right, Tan,' says Mr Lamble.

'Yes, that's right,' I say, and I hurry away. It was nice of him to tell me. But I've always been good at finding my way around.

There are kids everywhere in my new classroom. They are sitting on tables and standing on chairs and leaning against the pegs. They are all very … jumbly. Ted is over near the sports equipment and this is a big surprise for me. I did not know Ted would be in my class. He is pumping up a soccer ball and laughing and talking and pretending he doesn't know I am here. But he does.

'Tan!' says a voice.

I look around. It's Lily! She's standing by the pegs.

'Hang your backpack here,' says Lily, 'then you can sit at my table. I've got a spare seat.' Lily zips up her pencil case. It is a surfer girl pencil case with orange and pink flowers. 'That's Cindy and that's Grace,' she says, pointing to two other girls. 'They sit at my table, too.'

I smile at Cindy and Grace, but they ignore me. Cindy

is tall with big teeth at the front and a tight ponytail; Grace has stubby legs, freckles and a rainbow headband that is quite nice. I like headbands, but they don't always look good in my hair. It is too short and tufty.

'I can tell you everything you need to know about every kid in this school,' says Lily as she leads me across the room. 'I can tell you everything you need to know about the teachers, too. I've been at this school all my life and I know everything about everyone. Do you like our mouse?'

There is a cage on top of the tubs cabinet. Something pink and white is moving around in it.

'His name's Stuart,' says Lily. 'Ugly, isn't he?'

It is unfortunate, but I have to agree with Lily. Stuart is a very ugly mouse. His fur is patchy, his face is scaly and he has a twitch.

'What's wrong with him?' I say, poking my finger in the cage.

Stuart throws straw over himself.

'Bad nerves,' says Lily quietly. 'He's always worse at the beginning of term.'

'Oh,' I say.

'Ah-choo!' A high-pitched sneeze comes from outside the window.

'Quick!' says Lily. 'That's Miss Dragone. We had her last year. She shouts more than anyone in this whole school. You don't want to make enemies with Miss Dragone. She once had a fiancé. But he *disappeared*.'

Lily rushes to her chair.

Suddenly my stomach feels floaty again.

FIANCÉ: say, *fee-on-say*. A fiancé is a boyfriend who gives you a ring and then you say you will marry him and you tell everyone that he is your fiancé. It's a bit gross to think of a teacher having a fiancé.

Miss Dragone has very big ... boobs. I know it is rude to say things like that and it is even ruder to notice things like that.

But it is not possible to look at Miss Dragone and not see her **great big boobs.** Miss Dragone also has a big nose and big hair. She has big hands, too. She wears big earrings and big shoes and a big belt with a big silver buckle around her big dress. Everything about Miss Dragone is BIG.

'Good morning, class,' bellows Miss Dragone.

'Good mor ... ning, Miss Dra ... go ... neee.'

'How lovely to see your smiling faces again,' says Miss Dragone. 'What a treat to be together for another year.'

Miss Dragone looks around and everyone holds their breath and stands up straight. From where I am, I can see Stuart. He is shaking under his straw.

'Be seated,' says Miss Dragone.

We collapse onto our chairs. Lily hands me a note. It says:

Good morning,
Miss Dragonbum.

I don't know why, but Lily's note cracks me up. I can't help it. It is a hilarious piece of writing. I am trying so hard not to laugh that I snort.

'Hello ...' says Miss Dragone, looming over me. 'We have a new girl. A new girl with the snorts. Perhaps you would like to share your joke, Miss Callahan?' Miss Dragone has her hands on her hips.

'No, thank you, Miss Dragone,' I whisper. 'I would not like to share it.'

'Then I suggest you keep your snorts to yourself,' she says. 'You don't want to give me the wrong impression now, do you?'

'No, Miss. I don't.'

'As for you, Lily Pitt,' says Miss Dragone.

'Yes, Miss Dragone?' says Lily.

'I hope you will be mindful of Miss Callahan and not lead her astray,'

'Oh, no, Miss Dragone. I will be very mindful,' says Lily.

Miss Dragone goes back to the front and Lily gives me a wink. It is a very relieving wink and I like Lily even more because of it.

While Miss Dragone is taking the roll, I look around at

all the kids. They don't look much like country kids to me. Emerald told me country kids wear overalls and have no chins and teeth like old piano keys and chew on bits of straw. But I think Emerald tells lies. No one in this classroom is chewing straw – except for Stuart, and he's a mouse.

'Tan Callahan?'

'Yes, Miss Dragone?'

'Are you present or absent?'

'Um, present, Miss Dragone.'

'Very good.'

I notice Miss Dragone's earrings are shaped like cats. Big silver cats with twirling tails. I think this is a good sign. I think if Miss Dragone is a cat lover, she will be truly stunned and amazed by my Show and Tell. She will probably give me a gold star. It will be helpful to be popular with Miss Dragone.

There are heaps of kids with Show and Tell this morning. Everyone wants to talk about what they did on the holidays or what they saw or what they bought. It goes on and on. Someone has a faulty Shrek doll they won in a crane game.

The Shrek doll is cross-eyed and will probably be a collector's item one day. Someone else has fake vomit and Miss Dragone says it is very immature. Another kid has a squashed piñata from her brother's birthday. There is not one single lolly left in the piñata and I think it is a poor Show and Tell. Some boy has a spring-loaded fly gun and a jar of dead flies. That boy must have had a very boring holiday. Then Lily shows her tattoo and Miss Dragone says she hopes it will be gone by tomorrow. Finally, it is morning recess and we file out.

'Did you bring something for Show and Tell, Tan?' says Miss Dragone.

'I did, Miss Dragone,' I say.

'Very good. You can be first after recess. I'd like you to tell us a little about yourself.'

'Yes, Miss Dragone,' I say. Then I have an idea. 'Excuse me, Miss Dragone ...'

'Yes?'

'Could I have some private time to set up my Show and Tell?'

'Of course, Tan,' says Miss Dragone. 'It sounds mysterious.'

'Oh, it is, Miss Dragone. It's secretly mysterious.'

When the room is empty, I get out my cat skeleton. It has travelled well, although the tail needs some fixing. I stand it on a small table at the front of the classroom and lay the silk scarf over it. The cat skeleton is now completely hidden and it looks very … intriguing. I am excited to get started. But first I have to go to recess. I hope I can find Lily.

※ ※ ※

'Right, class,' says Miss Dragone, when we get back, 'I would like you to meet Tan Callahan. She is our new girl. She comes to us all the way from the city. And now that she knows a little about each of you, she would like tell you something about herself. Please sit quietly. Fidgeters will be evicted.'

EVICTED: this means chucked out or asked to wait in the corridor. I have been evicted from several classrooms, but it was never my fault.

I begin. 'My name is Tan Callahan and I have been living here for … not long, and I have three sisters, two dogs, one cat and a tortoise named Queen Victoria who I did not bring for Show and Tell.'

I think it is going well. Everyone is looking at the disguised cat skeleton and being fascinated. No one has been evicted either. My audience loves me. Except Ted. He is passing notes to his silly friends and ignoring me. It is time to raise my voice …

'During the holidays we found a dead fox that was cursed, and we met a bad-mannered country boy, who had a sheep's skull and a snake that can boil your brain, and my sister took a photo of a dead ghost that was floating in the trees.'

Ted has shut up and he is frowning. He has turned as red as a raspberry icy pole. Miss Dragone is frowning, too. It is time to get on with it.

'Now it is time for my Show and Tell.' I stand beside the cat skeleton. All the kids lean forward. I take a corner of the silk scarf.

'Prepare to be amazed,' I say, and I rip the silk scarf off the cat skeleton. 'Ta da!'

'Argh!' Miss Dragone screams at the top of her lungs.

It is such a loud scream that it gives me a terrible fright. I jump and I bump the table and the cat skeleton leaps in the air and its head flies in one direction and its tail flies in the other direction.

The whole class holds its breath as the cat skull somersaults through the air, toward Miss Dragone. Miss Dragone is still screaming and she puts her hands in front of her face … and catches the head. Then she screams again and drops the skull on the floor. The skull splits in two. Some of its teeth fall out. I am not sure where the tail has landed.

For a moment everyone is quiet. Then the boy with the fly gun stands up and starts to clap really slowly. 'That was the coolest Show and Tell I have ever seen,' says the boy.

I look at Ted. He is falling about laughing. I look at Miss Dragone. She is not falling about laughing.

From where I am standing, I can just see Stuart. He is as stiff and still as a stiff dead mouse.

'What does it say?' I ask, trying to look over Dad's shoulder.

'It says you have a *morbid curiosity*,' says Dad, and he hands Miss Dragone's note to Mum.

'That's good, isn't it?' I say. 'It's good to have curiosity.'

'Hmm,' says Mum. 'You must have scared that poor teacher out of her wits, Tan. I hope you haven't got her offside already.'

'It was an accident,' I whisper. 'I wanted her to be stunned and amazed.'

'Sounds like she was,' says Dad.

'Maybe if I make her some toffee fudge, she'll overlook this little incident,' says Mum.

'What about the mouse?' I say. 'Miss Dragone says my Show and Tell gave Stuart a heart attack.'

'But the mouse lived, didn't he?' says Dad.

'Yes,' I say, 'but only after Lily threw water in his face.'

'Then the mouse didn't have a heart attack,' says Dad. 'He was probably just scared stiff by all the screaming. You said yourself he has bad nerves.'

Awesome walks in. He puts his paw on my knee.

'See,' says Mum, 'even Awesome knows you didn't mean it. How about I make you a delicious strawberry sundae?'

'With double cream?' I say.

'Absolutely,' says Mum.

Dear Diary

I am writing to you by the light of my singing pineapple lamp — you know, the one that lost its voice after two songs.

It is not easy being a new girl. It is not easy to find popularness. I wish I could go back to my old school, where I was an old girl and I knew exactly who to sit with and who to talk to and I had Molly to walk around with and eat lunch with.

The boy with the fly gun is called Scooter. Scooter sits up the back with Ted and a bunch of other kids. Lily says I should stay away from the kids up the back. She says they are weird.

Scooter said I could have a turn at his fly gun. But I said no. I did not want to kill anything. Especially after I nearly killed Stuart.

Dad gave me ointment for Stuart's patches and drops for his bad nerves. I truly hope we can help Stuart. It is not fair for him to be scared and also ugly.

Lily said Miss Dragone is jealous of her tattoo and she won't wash it off.

I am thinking about Miss Dragone's fiancé. I will open a **Missing Fiancés** file for him.

Dad said he can fix the cat skeleton.

Truly
Tan

Episode Five:

Emus, Teachers and Other Carnivores

7

'Look at this,' whispers Lily, and she passes me a photo under the table. It is a photo of a white horse. It has its mouth open and its ears back and it is a very frightening creature.

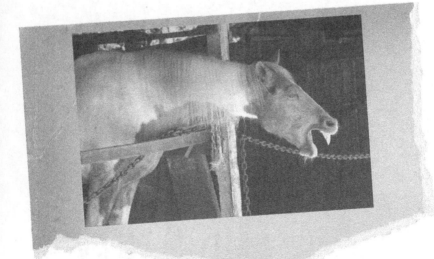

'His name's Casper,' says Lily. 'Isn't he beautiful? I got him last summer. I love horses. They're so beautiful and intelligent and ... *beautiful*. Do you love horses, Tan?'

I think for a moment. 'Oh, yes,' I say. 'I love horses. They are very nice animals. I don't have one myself ... but my dad has heaps of horse books and he has a horse on his desk. It's china. But its tail is real.'

'Enough chatter,' says Miss Dragone. She is drawing a food chain on the board.

I hold the photo on my lap and examine it closely. Casper has wild eyes and yellow teeth. Personally, I would be wary of Casper. It makes sense to be wary of a creature that can snap your leg with one snap or trample you with one trample. Some animals were designed to be avoided. These animals include crocodiles, vultures, red-bummed baboons ... and horses. I would also add domestic emus to this list.

DOMESTIC EMUS: these are emus that have been caught and made tame. They walk about quietly in their emu farms, but you should never, ever be fooled by a domestic emu. They will peck out your eyes as quick as look at you. I am sure of that.

'Tan Callahan, are you listening?' Miss Dragone is staring at me.

'Yes, Miss Dragone. I am listening.'

'Then tell me, what did I just say?'

'About what, Miss Dragone?'

'Can you give me an example of a carnivore, Miss Callahan?'

I look at Lily, but she shrugs her shoulders. I have to think quickly.

'I'm waiting, Miss Callahan …'

'The emu, Miss Dragone.'

'Excuse me?'

'The emu is a carnivore, Miss Dragone. Emus are large flightless birds. They have three toes, they can swim fast, they have cunning minds … and they are carnivores.'

Everyone starts laughing. Miss Dragone taps her foot.

'Ted Murphy, can you give us a definition of a carnivore?'

'A carnivore is a *meat-eating* animal,' says Ted.

'Correct,' says Miss Dragone. 'And can you give me an example, Ted?'

'Lions, tigers and wolves are carnivores,' says Ted, looking at me. 'Not *emus*.'

'Correct again,' says Miss Dragone. 'I'm glad someone has been paying attention.'

Rats! I could have sworn that emus were vicious hunters. Who would have thought they could grow that ugly and not eat meat?

Then Miss Dragone says, 'Tan Callahan, I have only known you two days, but already I am getting a poor impression.'

Ever since Monday and the little problem with the cat skeleton, Miss Dragone has been saying things like this to me. I think Miss Dragone might not like me. It is an uncomfortable feeling when your teacher doesn't like you. I know, because I have had this feeling before.

When the recess bell rings, Lily grabs my arm. 'Come on, let's get out of here,' she says. 'I've got a surprise.'

I can't wait to get outside and away from Miss Dragone. Plus, I am excited to know what Lily's surprise is. She wasn't on the bus this morning. This is the first time we have had a chance to talk properly.

Lily and I rush to get our snacks. Everyone is pushing and shoving at the pegs. Ted pushes in and pokes his tongue out at me. I poke mine back, because that is what you do. Suddenly Miss Dragone is beside me.

'I saw that, Tan,' she says.

'But he—' I start.

'You should not poke your tongue out at Ted just because he knows more than you,' says Miss Dragone.

Ted smiles at Miss Dragone.

'But he—' I start again.

'Do not interrupt me, Tan,' says Miss Dragone. 'I don't know what they taught you in the city, but here in the country we do not poke out our tongues.'

Miss Dragone has it all wrong. Everyone, everywhere, pokes out their tongues. It is a worldwide fact.

'You can stay in this recess, Tan,' says Miss Dragone. 'That will give you time to think about your manners. Off you go, Lily. Off you go, Ted.'

Lily grabs her playlunch and runs off with Grace and Cindy. Ted throws his soccer ball in the air, catches it and runs out.

The classroom is very quiet with just me and Miss Dragone. I sit at my table and open my playlunch. Miss Dragone sits at her desk and opens her playlunch. I can't see what she is eating. But I am sure Miss Dragone is a carnivore.

After I have eaten my triple-berry muffin and drunk my juice, I look around. Dum-dee-dum. Stuart is snuffling in his cage, but I decide to leave him alone. He is still recovering from his nervous attack. I smile at Miss Dragone, but she doesn't smile back. She opens a schoolbook and starts looking at it in a very important school-teacherish way. She has yellow chalk on her nose.

Outside, I can hear kids yelling and balls bouncing and I decide I am cross with Miss Dragone. I decide to write a poem. I get out a pencil and some paper.

Miss Dragone
makes me groaney
She's full of baloney
Her nose is bony
She's a big fat phoney
with a voice that's droney
That's Miss Dragone.

Hmm. Not bad. Who else can I write about?

There once was a boy called Ted
who should have been locked in a shed
He was rude
He was dumb
and a pain in the bum
That horrible boy called Ted.

Snap! Miss Dragone shuts her book and stands up.

'Well, Tan,' she says, coming over, 'it's nice to see you have had some quiet time. I hope it has been of benefit.'

'Oh yes, Miss Dragone. I'm sure it's a benefit.'

'Good,' says Miss Dragone. 'What are you writing?'

'Nothing, Miss Dragone … just my spelling words.'

'Well done, Tan. Let me see them.'

'What?'

'Let me see your spelling words, Tan.'

'Well, I, um …'

My heart has jumped into my throat and I know Miss Dragone will not like my poems. Even though they are excellent poems, I am sure she will not like them.

'Quickly now,' says Miss Dragone.

She holds out her hand. I try to smile nicely, but my cheeks are stiff and my teeth are stuck.

'Are you in pain, Tan?' says Miss Dragone.

'No, Miss Dragone,' I whisper. 'I'm not in pain.'

'Then hand me your spelling words.'

I pick up my poems and my heart beats fast and … *BRRRING.* The bell!

'Good heavens,' says Miss Dragone. 'Is it that time already?' She marches back to her desk.

Sometimes the bell rings just in time. Sometimes it is a lucky thing to have a bell.

When everyone comes back in, Lily is busy talking and laughing with Grace and Cindy and I can see that they have had fun at recess, and I have not.

'Have you been playing four-square?' I say to Cindy.

But Cindy just looks at me and laughs, and then Grace hands Cindy a piece of paper and Cindy laughs again. She passes the paper to me. On it there is a drawing of a crazy emu with big sharp teeth and eyes like purple gobstoppers. It says: Beware the Man-Eating Emu.

'Better watch out, Tan,' whispers Grace. 'Or the emus will get you!'

'Yeah,' says Cindy. 'They rip the heads off city kids!'

They all start laughing again. Even Lily. But I don't think it is a very funny joke.

'All right, all right!' yells Miss Dragone. 'Settle down, everyone. It's time we got on with our fascinating introduction to long division.'

Long division? Can today get any worse?

I drag out my maths book. I am still wondering what Lily's surprise is, but I don't feel like talking to her any more. And anyway, she is whispering to Cindy.

I stare out the window. The sun is shining and the sky is blue and I wonder what they are doing back at my old school. I bet they're not doing long division. Or stupid carnivores. Or being kept in at recess. Oh, yes, it was a nice old school, my old school …

8

'Finally,' says Miss Dragone, 'a quick brainteaser. A group of children set off on their bikes for a friend's house. The distance is fifteen kilometres. When they are two-thirds of the way, they stop for a rest. How far have they gone?'

Who cares how far they have gone? Obviously they have gone too far, if they have to stop for a rest. And why didn't one of the parents drive the kids the fifteen kilometres? That's the question I would ask, if I were the teacher.

Miss Dragone walks around the room, with her hands behind her back. I stare at my ruler. I do not want to catch Miss Dragone's eye. I do not want to answer her silly brainteaser. I am sick of maths. It is making me feel yawny.

Miss Dragone stops beside me. Her eyes bore into me, but I do not look up – not even for a nanosecond. It is like trying not to look when there's a giant yeti standing beside you, picking its nose. You are just busting to look, but you know that if you do, it will be a big mistake.

I keep my eyes fixed on the ruler. Miss Dragone taps

her foot. Then she says, 'Ted. Can you tell me the answer, please?'

Phew! Miss Dragone heads off down the back. Ha, ha, Ted. You won't have a clue.

'Psst,' says Lily, when Miss Dragone has her back to us.

'Yeah?' I say. I hope Lily does not want to discuss emus.

'Do you want to know my surprise?'

'Sure,' I say. 'What is it?'

'Mum said to see if you like horses.'

'Right,' I say, but I don't know why this is a surprise.

'She said you can come for a sleepover and we can go riding.'

'Riding?' I say carefully. 'Riding what?'

'Horses, silly!' says Lily.

'Oh,' I say.

'Well?' says Lily. 'What do you think? I can teach you everything I know about horses, which is a lot. We can ride and jump and it'll be the best fun.'

'But I don't have a horse,' I say.

'Doesn't matter,' says Lily. 'You can ride Rocket, my brother's horse.'

'Oh,' I say again.

'Trust me, you'll love it,' says Lily. 'We'll set up our own gymkhana.'

'Yeah,' I say slowly. 'I will definitely love that.' Then after a second I say, 'Tell me, is Rocket a very *big* horse?'

I am starting to feel sick. But what can I do? I like Lily and I think she is my new friend and I need a friend here in the country – even if it means I have to pretend about some things. Sometimes you just have to pretend. It is an important part of finding friends. It is an important part of finding popularness.

After school, I am relieved to be home. It's boiling hot and my hair is stuck to my head and my socks are cooking my feet and my backpack is as heavy as a camel's hump and there are three mozzy bites on the back of my knee that are itching like itching powder. It is an uncomfortable thing to be a school student in summer. This is true no matter where you live in the world.

Amber and Rose and I race each other up the steps, along the veranda and up to the flywire door that leads into the kitchen. We push through the door together and our backpacks get in a tangle and I fall over and Rose gets her foot hooked in my strap and Amber is yelling and Doodad is jumping around, yapping and panting and sniffing our backpacks. Inside, Babbles is beeping like a microwave, but Awesome is nowhere to be seen. Queen Victoria is snoozing under the kitchen table. Her head is hanging out of her shell and her nose is resting on the floorboards. She doesn't even wake up.

'Hopeless children,' says Emerald, and she steps over us and into the kitchen.

There is a note on the kitchen dresser. Amber lunges at it, but Emerald snatches it and reads it out:

Dear ones

I am in the attic, working.

Do not disturb me. I have made a jug of raspberry lemonade. It is in the fridge. The choc-chip cookies are also for you, my darlings. Tan, do not give any to Awesome. He has been particularly glum today. Chocolate will only add to his melancholy. See you at dinner.

Your loving mother

Coral Callahan

'What's melancholy?' I say as Rose throws open the fridge.

'It means he's a misery guts,' says Emerald, stuffing a cookie in her mouth.

'Oh,' I say. 'Is that all?'

I get myself a glass and wait for Rose. She is picking soggy raspberries out of the lemonade.

'Don't take them all!' says Amber.

Rose shoves a heap of raspberries in her mouth, mashes them up and opens her mouth wide.

'How gross!' says Amber.

'That's disgusting,' I say. It is disgusting and I think it is very funny.

Rose smiles and there is red gunge all over her braces and dribbling down her chin. **'I've come to suck your blood,'** she says, flapping her arms at Emerald.

'You are seriously immature,' says Emerald, and she flounces out of the room.

Emerald has been in year eight for three days and already she thinks she is a grown-up teenager. She thinks she is *mature* and *sophisticated*. But I know she is not mature and sophisticated, because I just saw her eat two choc-chip cookies at the same time.

When Emerald and Amber and Rose have all gone, I crawl under the kitchen table and tap on QV's shell. 'You awake, QV?' I whisper. 'I've got something for you.'

QV lifts her head slowly and opens one eye.

'Here you go,' I say, and I hold a fresh ripe raspberry in front of her nose.

QV stands up like an excited wonky tortoise and blinks at me. I can tell she is thinking that I am the nicest tortoise owner in the world. She gently takes the raspberry from my fingers and chomps into it. A line of juice trickles all the way down her wrinkly neck.

'QV, you are the most sophisticated person in this whole house,' I say. And that is the truth.

Up in World Headquarters, E is missing and I still haven't spotted Awesome anywhere. It is a bit of a mystery, but I will have to deal with it later. Right now I have to consult the

Magic 8 Ball. I am troubled because I have had a troubling day and I need some advice.

'Magic 8 Ball,' I say, 'will I have fun when I go horse riding with Lily?'

I close my eyes and shake the Magic 8 Ball.

BETTER NOT TELL YOU NOW, it says.

This is not a satisfactory answer. I shake the Magic 8 Ball again. 'Oh, great Magic 8 Ball,' I say, 'you are wise and all-knowing. Please tell me, will I be a good horse rider and a best friend of Lily after our sleepover?'

CONCENTRATE AND ASK AGAIN, says the Magic 8 Ball.

The Magic 8 Ball is making me cross. The stupid Magic 8 Ball is being … elusive.

ELUSIVE: sometimes it is hard to get a straight answer from someone, because they are being elusive. Sometimes it is hard to be friends with someone, because they keep slipping away and being elusive. Lily was being elusive today. Especially when Grace and Cindy were around.

'Magic 8 Ball,' I say, 'this is the last time I will ask … and you better answer properly because that's your job.'

I close my eyes tight and give the Magic 8 Ball a serious shake. 'Magic 8 Ball, is it a good idea for me to go horse riding with Lily?'

I open my eyes and the answer is … **MY SOURCES SAY NO.**

Now I know why the Magic 8 Ball was being elusive.

I flop down on the red beanbag. I just can't think about horses or Lily any more. I open an old book Mum gave me. It is about a girl called **Casey Kelvin, Girl Detective**. So far I have only read the first chapter, but I am not gripped.

I turn to chapter two, but it is hot in World Headquarters. It's quiet, too. Where *is* E? And more serious than that, where is Awesome?

I toss Casey Kelvin aside and climb down the ladder. Sorry, Casey. Tan Callahan has her own mysteries to solve.

I look everywhere. I check the love swing that hangs under the willow tree. Awesome enjoys sleeping there. But not today. I check the hidey-hole in the hedge, behind the front steps, inside the old machinery shed, under the tank stand.

All the places he likes. But still no Awesome.

What if he's run away? What if he's trying to get back to the city? He'll never, ever make it. It's too far, even for a dog as clever as Awesome. He'll end up like one of those hobo dogs you see in American movies. The ones that pad down dusty trails with sore paws and ribs that stick out. The ones that sleep in dumpsters and live off the kindness of strangers. The ones that save the lives of little children, but never stop anywhere long enough to find a true home. It's such a long, lonely, painful life. Poor Awesome!

'Awwwwwe...some!' I stand on the back veranda and call his name as loud as my voice box can yell. 'Awwwwwe...some! Come home!'

Rose wanders out onto the veranda. 'What's up?' she says.

'Awesome's run away!' I say, and I can feel my eyes watering. It must be the bright sun. 'I've looked everywhere.' I shade my eyes and stare at the empty horizon. 'Mum said he was extra melon ... extra mella ... extra *glum* today. Now he's gone. He's run away for sure!'

'No way,' says Rose, and she puts her arm around me. 'Awesome's too lazy to run away. Come on. I think I know where he is.'

Rose leaps down the veranda steps two at a time and heads off across the grass, through the hedge and toward the paddocks beyond.

It is a rare thing for Rose to put her arm around me. It is a rare thing for Rose to care about Awesome. But as I said, Rose is unpredictable.

I am wearing thongs and they are not designed for hurrying. I hobble through the paddocks after Rose. It is not easy to hurry through country paddocks. They are not smooth like city footpaths. They are lumpy and uneven and they have surprising little holes that bend your thongs and twist your ankles.

'Where are we going?' I say, when I catch up to Rose.

'To the dam,' says Rose.

Now this is news to me. I didn't even know we had a dam.

'You didn't even know we had a dam, did you?' says Rose.

It is a creepy thing, but Rose can **read minds.** I think I should wear a hat when I am around her so I can protect my mind from her Rose-rays.

We climb a small hill where there is no grass, just hard

crumbly dirt, and when we get to the top, I look down. Before us is a great big dam full of twinkling brown water.

'Awesome,' I gasp. Awesome is in the middle of the dam, swimming around and biting at water bugs. He looks up. I can tell he has recovered from his glumness.

I run down to the water's edge. I am so relieved to see my dog! I kick off my thongs and step into the shallows. The slimy mud squelches between my toes. But I don't care.

'Awesome!' I yell. 'You didn't run away!'

Awesome swims toward me. Then suddenly, *splat!* Something hits the back of my neck. I swing around. *Splat!* It's Rose and she is throwing great clumps of sticky mud at me!

'Hey,' I say. 'Cut it out!'

I bend over to get my own mud. But Rose leaps at me and gives me a shove. I fall face-first into the water. I kick and splutter and scoop huge globs of mud from under the water and hurl them at Rose.

splat! One gets her square on the chin. Rose looks like the bearded lady. What a brilliant shot.

I struggle to my feet, both fists loaded with mud. But Rose is too quick. She bombs me twice – *splat, splat* – then she leaps at me. I wrestle her and we both fall in the water, kicking and screaming.

By this time, Awesome has reached the shallows. He stands beside us and shakes water and mud everywhere.

Rose heaves herself out of the water and rubs mud all over her face and all through her long black hair.

'**Run, girl,**' she growls, 'for I am the mud zombie and I will suck out your brains and gnaw your bones.'

I scream and plough through the water. But Rose keeps coming at me, her arms sticking out in front like a stiff, dead zombie.

I stop for a second and swoosh water over her. But Rose just laughs.

'You think water can stop the mud zombie?' she howls.

'Get her, Awesome!' I yell, but Awesome is too busy scratching his wet collar and flicking his ears.

It is time to stand and fight. I cover myself with thick grey mud. It's in my hair and down my neck and shoulders and arms. Pretty soon all you can see of me is my eyes and my teeth.

'*Rar!*' I roar. 'I am an orc and I will feast on your tasty flesh, Rose Callahan!'

I lurch at Rose and I know that I do look like an orc, because Rose starts screaming.

It is the best mud fight I have ever had. It is the only mud fight I have ever had.

On the way back to the house, I say, 'Rose, what's a gymkhana?'

'It's something to do with horses,' says Rose, picking mud out of her ear. 'I think it's a competition where you set up jumps and obstacles and stuff.'

'Right,' I say. Then I say, 'Can you ride horses, Rose?'

'Never tried,' says Rose. 'Has someone asked you to go riding?' Rose is reading my mind again.

'Yes,' I say. 'I am going riding with Lily the weekend after next ... and the Magic 8 Ball said it is a bad idea.'

'Ha!' says Rose. 'Are you still using that Magic 8 Ball? I've told you before it's a rip-off. It's not even magic.'

'Well, I don't know about that,' I say, scratching my mozzy bites.

'Personally, I think palm reading is more reliable,' says Rose, and she grabs my hand and studies it. 'Hmm,' she says, frowning.

'What is it?' I whisper. I hope my palm doesn't say I will fall off a horse when I am in grade four and crack my skull open.

'You're going to have three husbands,' says Rose. 'No wait. Three children. Or maybe it's three cats. Anyway, there's nothing about horses on your palm, so it mustn't be important.'

'Does it really say all that?' I say, staring at my palm. I am truly amazed. All I can see is mud.

❋ ❋ ❋

Dear Diary

I am writing to you by the light of my electric

mosquito zapper — you know, the one that goes,

Snap! Crackle! Pop!

Awesome is snoring in his basket. He is tired.

Swimming makes you tired. So do mud fights.

Good night.

Truly
Tan

P.S. E came back. We don't know where
he went, but he had mud on his paws.

Episode Six:

Rumpled Notes, Coloured Sand and Krakens

9

The door to the school bus sighs and folds open. I slowly climb the steps.

'Hurry up, Tan,' says Amber. 'We haven't got all day.'

'She can't hurry,' says Emerald. 'Her bag's full of Dad's horse books. She's been reading them all weekend.'

'Oh, la-de-dah,' says Amber. 'I didn't mean to hurry little Miss Saddle Club.'

'Very funny,' I say, but I don't care what Amber says. She's just jealous, because she's scared of horses and I am not.

I dump my backpack on the seat and sit by the window. I can't wait for Lily to get on the bus. We'll have so much to talk about. She will love these horse books and we will definitely be best friends when she sees them. I think I will like being a horsey country girl. Maybe.

The bus chugs along. Ted and Jem get on. Jem squeals and throws her hands in the air and makes a huge fuss when she sees Amber – and Amber does exactly the same thing. It's as if they haven't seen each other for two years, not two days.

Amber and Jem are the biggest show-offs on this bus.

Ted walks past me and nods. This is unusual for Ted. He's not usually that friendly. He goes to the back of the bus and starts scribbling in a notepad.

After that, some other kids, who live on a dairy farm, get on and they are fighting over an action figure. The bus driver, Mr Pizzey, tells the kids to cut it out and sit down or he will throw the action figure out the window – and this is the truth. Mr Pizzey would definitely do that. Then Emerald's new friend Miranda gets on and I know that Emerald will be fuming because Miranda has a brand-new pink iPod Touch.

I am getting excited now. Lily's stop is next. I climb up and roll back the window. I try to stick my head out, but the window is too small and I can't fit my head through such a small space. Mr Pizzey yells into his bus microphone. 'Tan Callahan, quit fiddling with the windows and sit down!' Mr Pizzey has learned my name very quickly.

Lily's stop is just ahead. But the bus doesn't even slow down. It just zooms straight past. Rats! Lily mustn't be coming on the bus today. I truly hope she will be at school. I sigh and look out the window. But there are no tall buildings with rude graffiti, no crowded trams, no shifty people in dark glasses. There are only trees and paddocks and sheds and cows. Mr Pizzey should get a DVD player for this bus …

Plop. A ball of paper hits the back of my head and lands on the seat beside me. I look around, but I can't tell who has thrown it. If you ask me, everyone on this bus looks suspicious – even Mr Pizzey.

I unrumple the paper. It is a note. I smooth it out on my lap. It says:

URGENT MEETING AT
PH THIS SATURDAY NIGHT

It will be a sleepover.
Bring food. Bring torches.
Bring sleeping bags.

Bring the BIG dog but NOT the
little dog. Bring the box brownie.

REMEMBER: this is an urgent
meeting.

It is also TOP SECRET.

From, Ted

P.S. Bring the little dog if you
have to.

An urgent meeting at Purple Haunt! But I have horse riding with Lily this weekend. This is trouble. Big trouble. How can I say no to Lily? It is my strong feeling that Lily will not be my friend if I say no to horse riding. But I can't miss an urgent meeting at Purple Haunt either. What will I do? Sometimes you get on a bus and suddenly you have huge problems.

I look around. Emerald, Amber and Rose are all reading crumpled notes.

When the bus gets to school, I am still thinking about Ted's mysterious note. Why has he called an urgent meeting? Why does he want the box brownie? And how come we have to sleep over? Not that I think a sleepover at PH is a bad idea. It is an excellent idea.

'What did your note say?' I whisper to Rose as we climb down the bus steps.

'Shh,' says Rose. 'We'll talk about it tonight.'

'I see,' I whisper. 'So your note was top secret, too?'

'Remember the circle of truth,' says Rose, and she runs off.

Ted walks past me, but he doesn't nod this time. He doesn't even look at me. And I know why. It is because Ted does not want to blow his cover. He does not want to draw attention to himself or to the Chosen Few. Ted is shadowy and crafty. He would make a good secret agent. But I still don't like him.

Lily is hanging her bag on the pegs.

'Hi!' I say. 'You weren't on the bus.'

'I know,' says Lily, but she is not looking at me. She is standing on tippy-toes, peering into the crowded corridor.

Ted tries to throw his bag on a peg, but it skids across the floor and a grungy apple bounces out and rolls between a group of girls who are trying on glitter gloss. The girls kick the apple to Grace and Cindy and they kick it to me and I kick it to Ted. Ted catches it and pretends he is puking. The apple is spongy and fusty and it is my guess it is a last-term apple. Morning music blasts over the loud speaker. It is getting busier by the second.

'I brought all these amazing horse books,' I say as I peel off my backpack. 'For us to look at.'

'Good,' says Lily quickly, then she gasps and jumps in the air and waves frantically. 'Over here!' she cries. 'Verity! I'm over here!' Lily pushes past me and into the corridor.

I hang up my bag and open the zipper. I pull out my pencil case. I dig around for my ruler and dictionary – and all the time I am wondering who Verity is. I have not met anyone in our class called Verity. Maybe she is a new girl?

Then Grace and Cindy squeal, 'Verity!' and they rush into the corridor, too. It is then that I know Verity is not a new girl. It seems everyone knows her. Except me.

I go to class, dump my stuff on my chair, and check on Stuart.

'Remarkable, isn't it?' says a girl who is peering into Stuart's cage.

'Yes,' I say, and it is remarkable. Stuart's fur is growing back and he is nowhere near as twitchy.

'It was the medicine your dad gave us. It's quite magical,' says the girl, lifting Stuart out and tickling his head. Stuart panics, runs up her arm and starts cleaning his head.

'Who are you?' I say to the girl.

'I'm Gloria,' she says. 'I enjoyed your Show and Tell last week. I've always found anatomy fascinating.'

'I'm Tan,' I say. 'I sit with Lily and Grace and Cindy.'

'I know,' says Gloria. 'I sit up the back with Ted and Scooter and Angus. They're good at soccer and drawing.

123

I'm really good at science and I make necklaces.'

It is a complicated thing, but I have tried not to take too much notice of the kids up the back. Not since Lily said they were weird. Not since Grace and Cindy said they were hopeless. Not since I knew Ted sat with them.

Gloria giggles. Stuart is trying to hide in her hair.

'Here, I'll catch him,' I say. 'But you'll have to hold still.'

Gloria has thick black hair in lots of plaits and I have to be careful. Stuart could get tangled in there. Then we would have to cut him out and that would be ugly.

I drag Stuart out of Gloria's hair and place him in her hand.

'Phew. Thanks, Tan,' she says, and she sits Stuart back in his cage. He hops in his wheel and spins like a maniac. He looks like a normal little uptight mouse – except for when his eyelid jitters.

Gloria has a necklace with wooden cubes that spell GLORIA.

'Did you make that?' I say, nodding at the necklace.

'Yes, I did,' says Gloria. 'This is one of my most popular designs.'

'It's very artistic,' I say.

We watch Stuart for a second, then Gloria looks over her shoulder. 'Uh oh,' she whispers. 'Verity Crisp is back. Will the horror ever end? See you later, Tan.'

Gloria is an odd girl. But I don't think she is weird. And I don't think she is hopeless. I watch her closely as she heads down the back.

Then I turn to face Verity Crisp.

10

Verity Crisp wears a watch. It is see-through with a pink-and-white striped band. She is small – even smaller than me. But she has lots of hair. It is brown and swirly and she has a hairclip either side of her head. The hairclips have sparkly silver butterflies with fake diamonds on their wings. It is not such a nice thing to say, but Verity Crisp reminds me of Doodad.

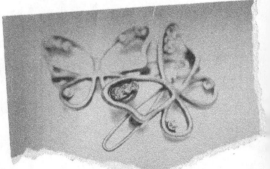

'Is this your stuff?' says Verity. She is standing by my chair with Lily. Lily is looking at her feet. Verity is looking at me. She is holding my pencil case and my ruler and my dictionary.

'Yes, thank you,' I say, taking my things. 'This is my stuff and this is my chair.'

'I don't think so,' says Verity. 'This is my chair. You'll have to take your stuff and sit somewhere else.'

'I don't think so,' I say. Grace and Cindy stop what they are doing and listen. 'I have been sitting here for a week,' I say calmly. 'So this is my chair.'

Verity puts her hands on her hips and her face goes red. Her butterflies jiggle. I think I would like to whack her with my ruler.

Lily puts her hand on my arm. 'Sorry, Tan,' she says quietly. 'This really is Verity's chair. She always sits at our table. She's class captain.'

Verity taps the gold badge on her collar.

'So what if she's class captain?' I say. 'She can't come in here and push people out of their chairs. Just because she's class captain doesn't mean she owns the chairs.'

Grace and Cindy gasp. Verity flips the chair around.

'If you've been here a week, how come you haven't noticed this?' she says.

Across the back of the chair the letters VC are written in curly red paint.

'Well, that could mean anything,' I say. 'It probably means … Vinyl Chair or … Vanilla Custard or … or … *Very Crazy.*'

Lily laughs, but Verity frowns at her and she stops laughing straight away.

Verity plonks herself down and crosses her arms. 'This is my chair and I'm not moving,' she snaps, and she sticks her nose in the air.

Maybe I should tip her out? That would be a reasonable thing to do. The others are staring at me. Someone has to do something. I reach out, grab the back of the chair and—

'Verity!' Miss Dragone booms into the room. 'You're back! Did you have a wonderful holiday? We've all missed you so.'

'Yes, Miss Dragone,' says Verity, jumping up and smiling sweetly. 'I had a wonderful holiday. I brought you back a gift.'

Verity reaches into her pocket and hands Miss Dragone a small bottle. It has a blue plastic lid and it is full of brown and red and gold zigzags.

'It's coloured sand, Miss Dragone,' says Verity. 'It's extremely rare.'

'How lovely,' says Miss Dragone, holding the bottle up. 'I shall cherish it. Now come along. You can tell us all about your travels. We're dying to hear it all.'

Miss Dragone turns to the class and claps her hands. Verity pokes her tongue out at me.

'Everyone to their chairs, NOW!' calls Miss Dragone.

'Verity has surprised us by coming back early and now she's going to tell us all about her trip.'

'Excuse me, Miss Dragone.'

'Yes, Tan. What is it?'

'Um. I don't have a chair.'

I scowl at Verity, but she is busy clipping purple butterflies in Lily's hair. They are ugly butterflies and I can't believe Lily would want them in her hair.

'Hmm. Now, where to put you ...' says Miss Dragone, pursing her lips.

'She can sit with us,' someone calls.

I swing round. It's Gloria. She gives me a quick wave. 'We've got a spare chair,' she says.

Grace and Cindy start whispering behind their hands.

'Yeah,' says Scooter, standing up. 'Tan can sit with us. We've got a spare chair.'

Grace and Cindy burst into giggles.

'Hush!' says Miss Dragone, and Grace and Cindy sit up. 'Yes, yes. Off you go, Tan. Down the back. But remember, no nonsense. Do you understand?'

'Yes, Miss Dragone,' I say as I gather my things. 'I understand.'

Verity's Show and Tell is the longest in the history of the planet Earth. She talks for hours. Even Miss Dragone yawns.

'... and after that I had two lessons with Julian and then I knew exactly how to snorkel and he said I was the best student he'd ever had and I snorkelled around everywhere and I saw many beautiful fish and coloured coral and ... *blah, blah, blah.*'

'Wish she'd seen a shark,' mutters Ted.

'Or a killer whale,' says Scooter.

'Or a kraken,' says Gloria.

'What's a kraken?' I whisper, and I am careful that Miss Dragone can't see me.

'It's a giant monster of the deep,' whispers Gloria.

'It's like a gigantic squid with huge slimy tentacles and a mouth the size of a football oval,' says Ted. 'I'm really good at drawing them.'

'Cool,' I say, and in my mind I can see a kraken swallowing Verity Crisp and licking its lips and spitting her sparkly butterflies and her gold badge high into the air. It is a lovely picture to have in my head.

'... and then we caught the plane home and I wore my new sarong, which is a floaty sort of dress that everyone wears on tropical islands and—'

'Yes, yes,' says Miss Dragone, resting her hands on Verity's shoulders. 'Bravo. Bravo. Now you're back with us and we're very pleased to see you. Everyone, give Verity a round of applause and thank her for a fascinating Show and Tell.'

Everyone in the class claps and cheers and Ted does a high-pitched whistle. Verity takes a sweeping bow.

She thinks we are clapping because we enjoyed her talk. But I am sure we are clapping because we are so happy her talk is *over.*

Verity goes back to her seat and Lily is smiling and happy and whispering something in Verity's ear … and it is then that I realise something. Lily likes Verity a lot more than she likes me. I have to look away.

At recess, Lily and Grace and Cindy race outside with Verity, and I have to run to catch up. When I find them, they are playing four-square.

'Wow,' I say. 'Looks like a fast game.'

'Sorry, Tan,' says Lily, whacking the ball. 'We don't need extras.'

'That's right,' says Cindy, bending over to catch her breath. 'Four's enough for *four*-square.'

Grace starts giggling.

'More than four people can play four-square,' I say, crossing my arms. 'We did it all the time at my old school.'

Verity catches the ball. 'Who cares what you did at your old school?' she says, and she flicks her hair.

'Yeah, who cares?' says Cindy.

'See you later, Tan,' says Verity as she serves to Lily. 'Have fun with Gloria.'

'Yeah,' says Grace. 'Have fun with *Ted*.'

They all start laughing. I look at Lily, but she just ignores me and keeps hitting the ball. I notice that she is still wearing the horrible purple butterflies in her hair. Suddenly I am glad that Lily looks stupid.

After that, I decide to go to the library. Libraries are good places when you are on your own and you feel like the weirdest kid in the history of school.

The library is cool and quiet and there are paintings by prep kids all down one wall. I walk along and look at the paintings. There is one of a dog, but its legs look like toothpicks and its body looks like a hamburger bun.

'Hello, Tan,' says a friendly voice. It is Mr Lamble. Today his bow tie is navy with yellow spots.

'How are you enjoying Peppercorn Grove?' he says. 'Fitting in nicely?'

'It's a very nice school, Mr Lamble,' I say. 'It's easy to fit in.'

'Wonderful,' says Mr Lamble, beaming. 'So why are you in the library on such a glorious morning?'

'Um. I'm doing research, Mr Lamble.'

'Research?' says Mr Lamble, and he takes off his spectacles and gives them a polish. 'Well, I admire that, Tan. What are you researching?'

'Oh, the ... um ... kraken.'

'Gracious me,' says Mr Lamble. 'The kraken, hey? I know just the book.'

Mr Lamble leads me to the section marked NON-FICTION. He pulls out a big book with ships and pirates on the cover.

'Enjoy your research, Tan,' says Mr Lamble, and he heads off to the teacher's lounge.

I find myself a seat and open the book ...

No sea monster has ever been as horrifying as the kraken.

This huge, many-armed creature would wrap its tentacles around a ship and crush it. The crew would be eaten by the monster or crushed to death ...

'Hi Tan. What're you reading?'

'Oh. Gloria. Hi. I'm just, you know, reading about the kraken.'

'Really?' says Gloria. 'Well, you've got the best book.'

'That's what Mr Lamble said.'

Gloria sits down and pulls up her socks. 'We were looking for you, Tan,' she says.

'Really?' I say. 'Well, I'm in the library.'

'Yes, I see that,' says Gloria.

There is a book about horses on the table. Gloria picks it up and flicks through it. After a minute, she tosses the book down. 'Yuk,' she says. 'I hate horses.'

'Do you?' I say, and this is interesting news. 'I don't hate them. Not exactly. But I don't love them either. I just think they're ... overrated.'

'Precisely!' says Gloria. 'Overrated and *monstrous*.'

Gloria grins. She has a big gap between her two front teeth. Something about her makes me feel happy and this is strange, because today has not been happy.

I am thinking all this when Gloria says, 'Aren't you friends with Lily any more?'

'I ... I don't know,' I say, studying a squid with a harpoon between its eyes. 'I was supposed to sleep over at her house this weekend and go horse riding. But she's a bit busy with Verity now, and I think the sleepover's off.'

'Hmm,' says Gloria. 'Does that really matter? Who wants to plod around a paddock on some four-legged monster anyway? You'd probably end up lying in the mud with a cracked skull.'

'I suppose …' I sigh.

'I could never be friends with someone like Verity,' says Gloria. 'Ted calls her Little Miss Prissy-Butterfly-Britches.'

I start to giggle. 'But what about Lily?' I say, straightening up. 'Why is Lily friends with her?'

'Who knows?' Gloria shrugs. 'They've been best friends forever. Their fathers work together. They own Ye Olde Real Estate Agents in town.'

'Really?' I say. 'Wow! There was someone who dropped dead—'

I stop suddenly. I do not want to say anything about Wandering Wanda. It might be a secret of the Chosen Few.

'What were you going to say?' says Gloria, and she looks as curious as **Casey Kelvin, Girl Detective.**

'Nothing,' I say quickly.

'Come on, Tan,' says Gloria. 'Come and play soccer with us. It can be you and me against the boys. We'll flatten them!'

But I don't have time to say yes, because just then the bell goes and we have to go back to class.

'Do you like my necklace?' says Gloria as we walk down the library steps. 'I could make you one, if you like.'

'Yes, I do like your necklace,' I say. 'And I think one with TAN on it would be beautiful.'

And that is the truth.

11

'So then she flipped the chair around and said it was hers because it had VC on it. Can you pass the potatoes, Rose?'

We are having dinner and everyone is listening to my story. Rose takes a scoop of olive mashed potato and pushes the bowl down to me.

'What does VC stand for?' says Amber, biting into a Spanish-style crumbed cutlet.

'It's her initials,' I say.

'Whatever,' says Emerald. 'She sounds hideous to me. Are you sure she's not on the bus? I could have a quiet word in her ear ...'

'Come along now, Emerald. We don't want you whispering in *anyone's* ear,' says Mum, sliding a slow-roasted tomato onto Dad's plate.

'That's right,' says Dad. 'Besides, it sounds like Tan handled it pretty well. When all's said and done.'

'Yes,' says Mum. 'When all's said and done.'

Mum and Dad often say weird things like that.

'VC,' says Rose, making swirls in her potato. 'VC. Now let me think. I bet it stands for ... *Violent Criminal.*'

'Ha!' says Emerald. 'Good one, Rose. But I've got a better one. *Vengeful Child.*'

'Impressive,' says Rose, nodding, and she gives Emerald a high five.

> VENGEFUL CHILD: a vengeful child is a child who does mean things to get at people, like stealing other kids' chairs or being a four-square bully.

'Verity Crisp,' I say, cutting myself a slab of homemade rosemary soda bread.

'Hmm?' says Mum.

'That's her name. Verity Crisp.'

'Poo,' says Amber. 'What kind of a name is that? That's a silly name for a silly girl.' Amber adjusts her tiara. It keeps slipping over her eyes.

'Crisp,' says Mum, putting down her fork. 'Isn't that the name of that awful estate agent who likes to hunt? The one who hung the dead fox over the fence post?'

'Yep,' I say. 'That's her father.'

'Well,' says Mum, flicking her napkin. 'Say no more!'

And that's what we do. We say no more about Verity Crisp. But I do tell them about Gloria, and Emerald says she sounds cool, and Dad asks if she has any pets, and Amber says she can't understand a girl who likes science and plays soccer. Rose doesn't say anything, because she is slipping bread and jam to Awesome and Mum would have a fit if she knew.

Dear Diary

I am writing to you by the light of my reptile
incubation lamp — you know, the one that is also
chicken friendly. Today was horrible. It was even more
horrible than my first day. I was very sad to see Lily go
off with Verity. Emerald said Lily is obviously fickle.
I looked up 'fickle'. It means changing your mind a lot.
I have changed my mind about Lily — I don't think
she's so nice any more, so I guess I am fickle, too.
But I might change my mind about that.

After dinner, I sat on the love swing with Dad and he told me
about his friends at school, which was boring. Then he told
me he had a good feeling about Gloria, which was nice.

At bedtime, the lollipops sat on my bed and we
compared our rumpled Ted notes. They all said exactly
the same thing! Ted is such a rattle-brain. But we are
all excited about sleeping over at Purple Haunt.
Except Emerald. She says sleepovers with your sisters are lame.
But she is coming anyway.

It is a relieving thing to not go horse riding.
Truly
Tan

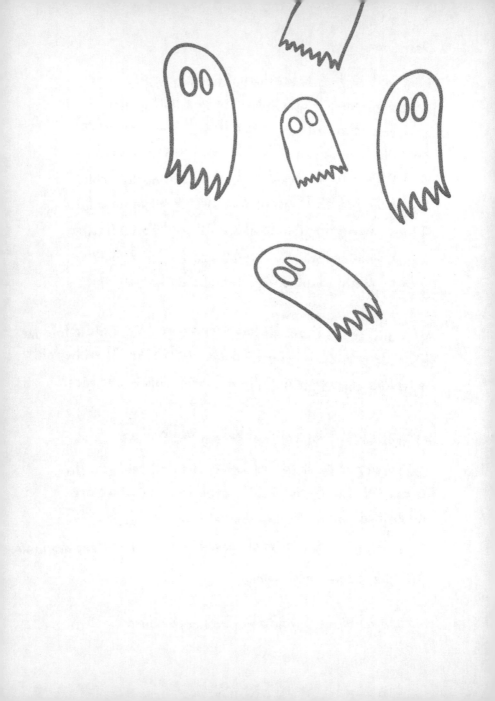

Episode Seven:

Sleepovers, Spooks and a Dark, Dark Dunny

12

'Ooh,' groans Amber as she peddles along. 'Do you really think we should be doing this? Maybe we could just visit. We could give Jem and Ted some cake, have the meeting and go home.'

'Don't be a wuss,' says Emerald, who is riding beside her. 'If I have to go on this stupid sleepover, then you do, too. Just be quiet and hurry up. We have to get there before dark or we'll end up lost in the bush and they'll have to send a helicopter to look for us.'

Emerald changes gear and zooms ahead. Amber peddles harder, but she can't keep up. She is finding it hard work riding to Purple Haunt tonight. She is finding it hard work because our bikes are loaded up and our backpacks are also loaded up.

This is what I have in my backpack: twenty-four sausage rolls, a bottle of tomato sauce, a cinnamon teacake, a tin of toffee brownies, a watermelon that has been cut up, a bag of jelly babies, my toothbrush, my roll-on mosquito killer, my army camouflage pyjamas and hat, my waterproof torch, my Spy 'n' Pry magnifying glass, my diary and a water pistol I forgot I had. On the back of my bike I have my sleeping bag and my favourite pillow.

Emerald also has a sleeping bag and a pillow and a backpack full of food and other important sleepover items. So does Rose and so does Amber. But Amber also has a collapsible chair, an airbed, an airbed pump and Doodad. Doodad is sitting at the front of Amber's bike, in a flowery basket. She is wearing a pink collar with fake diamonds and pearls and a matching *Diva Doggie* satin jacket. Doodad does not look like she is going to an urgent meeting. She looks like she is going to a Stupidest Dog competition. Awesome is keeping away from her. He does not want to be seen with such a ninny-dog.

'Have you got the box brownie?' I say to Rose as she peddles along beside me.

'Yes,' says Rose. 'That's the fiftieth time you've asked me.'

'Just checking,' I say loudly so Amber can hear. 'There has obviously been something paranormal going on at Purple Haunt. Why else would Ted ask us to bring the box brownie?'

Behind us we hear Amber whimper.

Rose looks up at the sky. "Twill be sunset soon,' she rumbles. **"Twill be sunset and the creatures of the night will be restless and *unquiet*.'**

'Shut up, Rose!' says Amber, coming up beside us. Doodad's head is lolling over the side of the basket. I think she feels seasick. But Amber doesn't notice. 'If you don't keep your big mouth shut,' she goes on, 'I'm going to turn my bike around and go straight home.'

"Twill be a long lonely ride, Amber Callahan,' rumbles Rose.

'Emerald,' whines Amber, 'tell her to shut up!'

'Quit it, Rose,' says Emerald. 'Remember what Mum said. *I'm in charge.'*

Rose speeds past us, her long black hair streaming behind her like shiny ribbons. She's wearing a black T-shirt with fake leopard fur around the neck, a long black skirt with a ragged hem, red-and-black striped tights and bright-pink gym boots with white laces. Rose knows a lot about the paranormal.

When we get to the dead fox fence post, we lean our bikes against the trees.

'Here, boy,' I say to Awesome. Awesome stands beside me like a patient horse who knows how to wait patiently.

I carefully strap my sleeping bag and pillow to his sides.

'You can't do that!' says Emerald.

'Why not?' I say, hoicking my backpack onto my back. 'Awesome and I are in this together. If I have to carry a load, so does he. He's my faithful companion and that's what faithful companions do.'

Emerald shakes her head and mutters something as she ties her sleeping bag to her backpack. I notice Amber looking a Doodad, but you could not even strap a coin purse to Doodad – especially when she is seasick.

'You will have to carry that animal,' I say to Amber. 'It does not look at all well.'

'I know,' grumbles Amber. 'She hates it when I ride fast.'

Amber unhooks the flowery basket. It has an extra strap so it can be carried like a shoulder bag. 'Come on, Doody,' she sighs as she drapes the basket over her shoulder. Doodad gives Amber a pathetic look and snuggles down behind the flowers.

With all her junk and her dog in a basket, Amber looks like a crotchety old bag lady. Rose and I try not to laugh as we follow Awesome into the bush and down the track to Purple Haunt.

Overhead, the cockatoos are screeching in the trees. Pink sky is peeking through the branches. The sun is setting. Soon it will be dark.

'Took your time,' says Ted as we finally step out of the bush and arrive at Purple Haunt. Ted is poking around down by the creek.

'It wasn't our fault,' says Emerald, throwing down her backpack. 'Our mother had to cook everything ever invented.'

'And then it took three hours to fit it all in,' says Rose, picking a prickle out of her tights.

'So you brought plenty of food?' says Ted, jabbing a long stick in the mud and coming over.

'Of course we brought food, Ted,' I say, unstrapping Awesome's load. 'That is what we just said.'

Awesome shakes himself and rolls in the dirt.

Ted scratches his belly. 'G'day mate,' he says. 'Good to see you again.'

Ted is still trying to make Awesome like him. But it will never work.

'Amber! Doody!' calls Jem, and she rushes down the steps of Purple Haunt. She hugs Amber and prises Doodad out of the flowery basket.

'I'm so glad you came, Doody,' says Jem, holding Doodad in the air. 'I was extremely cross with Ted for suggesting you weren't welcome.'

Doodad looks starry-eyed, but she does not look seasick any more. Amber, on the other hand, is as pale as a pale white crayon. She drops everything and flops against a tree.

'So, do we take our stuff up there?' says Emerald, nodding at Purple Haunt. 'Or do we sleep out here?'

'Never!' says Jem, smoothing Doodad's diva jacket. 'We wouldn't let our guests sleep outside.'

Emerald and Rose smirk.

'Follow me, Chosen Few,' says Jem briskly. 'Ted, assist

Amber with her belongings. You can put them in the parlour. Quickly now! She's exhausted.'

Ted grumbles, but he picks up Amber's stuff. Amber dabs her forehead with a hanky. 'I'll be there in a moment,' she says with a sigh.

We follow Jem and Ted up the steps. Purple Haunt has two big rooms, one at the front and one at the back. Jem calls the front room the *parlour*. The back room is the *drawing room*.

The parlour looks much the same as the last time we were here, except for two air mattresses with sleeping bags, which must be Jem's and Ted's. There are also two Eskies against one wall. In the middle of the floor, there is a fancy red-and-gold rug and a stack of brightly coloured cushions with tassels and gold braiding.

While Emerald and Rose fight about where they're going to sleep, I wander into the drawing room. Open shelves line the walls and they are loaded with treasures. The black-eyed brain-boiler is still here. It stares at me through the murky glass, looking deadly ... and dead.

There are also bird nests and rocks and cocoons and at least twenty different Barbie dolls (some of them are so old they have turned yellow). There are also sea sponges and cuttlefish and china elephants and soccer trophies and ballet trophies and feathers and a big clay head that looks like a caveman, and books and comics and *Dancing Queen* magazines. There is also a spiral-bound notebook, a mug of pens and a small brass bell.

I am just about to pick up the bell when Awesome starts barking like a guard dog. I run out to the veranda. Awesome is running up and down in the bushes, sniffing and wagging his tail. The branches part ... and Gloria steps out!

'Phew,' says Gloria, picking twigs out of her hair. 'I don't know how I got lost after all these years.'

Jem rushes down the steps and gives Gloria a hug. Ted is hanging over the veranda, watching.

'What's wrong with you?' he says, elbowing me in the side. 'Didn't you know Gloria was in the Chosen Few? She's our cousin, you know.'

I am shocked. I have been friends with Gloria for a whole week and all this time I did not know she was in the Chosen Few.

I did not know she was anyone's cousin either. I begin to wonder if there are other things I don't know about Gloria. Things that could be upsetting. I begin to wonder if Gloria is … fickle.

'Thank goodness I brought a compass,' says Gloria. 'I took the wrong trail and went round and round in circles and nearly got bamboozled.'

Gloria fiddles with the straps on her backpack then looks up.

'Tan!' She grins, and drops her backpack in the dirt. 'I knew you'd come!'

BAMBOOZLED: sometimes things happen that you just don't expect and inside your head your brain is going round and round and that is when you know you are bamboozled.

13

'Right,' says Ted, 'grab a cushion and sit down. I want to get this meeting started.'

We all gather around the picnic rug in the middle of Purple Haunt. I sit next to Gloria. Emerald is on the other side of me, then there's Rose, Ted, Awesome (who does not have a cushion), Jem and Amber. Doodad is asleep in Amber's lap.

Amber and Jem are giggling. Amber is feeling much better since she ate some sausage rolls and some chicken wings and two chocolate patty cakes. It is dark outside and there is no electricity in Purple Haunt, but there is a bright moon and zillions of stars and Jem has lit a tall red candle and it is glowing in the middle of the circle. We can easily see. Plus, we all have our torches in case of emergencies … or heebie jeebies.

Ted claps his hands suddenly. Amber and Jem stop giggling and Emerald turns off her MP3 player.

'I would now like to call to order this urgent meeting of the Chosen Few,' says Ted, and he rings the little brass bell.

'Would Emerald please pass the Jaffas?'

Emerald rolls two Jaffas across the rug to Ted. 'Two at a time,' she says. 'That's the rule.'

Gloria digs me with her elbow and I try not to laugh. Emerald thinks she is the Jaffa Queen, but she's not, because Gloria and I have snaffled our own secret stash. We have Jaffas AND jelly babies.

'Thank you,' says Ted. 'Jem, are you taking notes?'

'What? Oh. Yes,' says Jem, and Amber starts giggling again.

Jem opens the spiral notebook and clicks her pen and Rose starts whispering to Emerald and I start whispering to Gloria and Awesome starts scratching and Doodad starts wriggling. Ted rings the bell again.

'Silence!' he snaps. 'I have called you here tonight for a very important reason.' He looks slowly around the circle. 'I have called you here to discuss *the haunting of Purple Haunt.*'

The candle flame flickers. Everyone stops wriggling and whispering and giggling and suddenly it is absolutely totally silent in Purple Haunt. Outside, frogs are croaking. The night wind sighs. The veranda boards creak. In the distance, something is moaning … or mooing. Either way, I have my hand on my torch – and so does everyone else.

Then *BANG!* Emerald pops a chip bag and we all jump. Emerald laughs.

'Yeah, sure, Ted,' she says, poking her fingers into the chip bag. 'We've been through this before. Purple Haunt has a ghost. Blah-de-blah. Purple Haunt is haunted. Right. Good one.'

Emerald crunches on her chips. They're salt and vinegar. Awesome dribbles.

'It's true!' says Ted. 'I thought it was, you know, just nothing but then—'

'But then,' says Jem, dropping the spiral notebook, 'it all began to fall into place. There have been signs, Chosen Few. Signs too numerous to mention. And they all point to one thing. Wandering Wanda is haunting Purple Haunt!'

Amber gasps. Gloria looks at me and bites her lip.

'In fact,' whispers Jem, 'I suspect she is in this room right now, *listening*.'

'What?' squeals Amber, and she flicks on her torch. 'The ghost is in here now? How do you know? Where is she?'

Amber flashes her torch around frantically. 'What are we going to *do*?'

'Turn off that torch,' says Ted. 'Do you want to make the ghost angry?'

'Sorry,' squeaks Amber, and she jams the torch under her cushion.

Jem puts her arm around Amber and everyone starts talking at once. Even Emerald. Ted rings the bell over and over, but we all ignore him.

Then Rose lifts the red candle and holds it before her. Her face looms in the candlelight. It looks shadowy and out of shape and her hair dangles around her eyes like a frayed black veil. It's odd, but if she moves the candle up and down, her eyebrows look like they're going up and down, too. They're like big black moth's wings. It is a creepy thing to watch and I am looking forward to having a turn …

Then Rose begins to speak. She speaks softly and slowly. We have to be quiet and listen hard.

'Speak to us, Ted,' she says. 'Tell us your ectoplasmic tale and we will listen. For we are the Chosen Few and we are your companions in this time of paranormal unrest.'

There is silence for a moment. Then Gloria says, 'Wow! I wish I'd said that.'

'Rose always says stuff like that,' I say, stuffing two jelly babies and a Jaffa in my mouth.

Rose passes the candle to Ted. He looks at it for a moment.

'Hold the candle before you, Ted,' I say. 'The one who is speaking holds the candle before them. It is a common sleepover rule.'

SLEEPOVER RULES: not everyone knows this, but you can make up anything on a sleepover and say it is a common sleepover rule and everyone will believe you. I like that.

Ted gives me a 'you are such a pain' look. Then he holds the candle before him and this is what he tells us:

☀ He slept at Purple Haunt twice last weekend.
☀ He has visited every night after school this week.
☀ He has noticed many strange things.

These are the strange things he has noticed:

✳ The letterbox keeps falling over. Ted fixes it, but the next day it has fallen over again.

✳ There have been hundreds and thousands all over the floor – twice. And Ted has not been eating fairy bread.

✳ Jem's CD player blew up and her *Cats* CD buckled.

✳ Two crow feathers were jammed up the sheep skull's snout.

✳ But worst of all – yesterday, under the ghost gum, down by the creek, there were four sticks placed in the shape of a great big W.

Everyone starts yabbering again. It is obvious that Wandering Wanda is doing some serious haunting. We need to think carefully.

'Maybe we should spray garlic water everywhere?' I say.

'Oh, yes!' says Gloria. 'I read about garlic water once. It's very effective.'

'Or silver bullets,' says Amber. 'Silver bullets are good.'

'But we don't have a gun,' says Jem, looking worried.

'Man. Don't you guys know anything?' says Emerald, screwing up her empty chip bag. 'Those things are for *vampires*. Wandering Wanda's not a vampire ... she's just an ordinary flimsy ghost. You can't shoot ghosts or spray them with garlic water. It doesn't work.'

'So you do believe us!' says Ted.

'Maybe,' says Emerald, yawning. 'But I can't be bothered with it now. I'm going to bed.'

Emerald gets up, stretches and staggers over to her sleeping bag. 'Nighty-night,' she says as she crawls in. 'Don't let the Wandering Wandas bite.'

She plugs her MP3 player in her ears and rolls over. And that's the end of our urgent meeting.

We all sit there for a moment. Then Jem says, 'I'm astounded. How can she sleep under such harrowing conditions?'

None of us know how Emerald can sleep right now, but we decide the best thing is to put our sleeping bags in a circle and stick together for the night. We station Awesome in the middle of the circle. He is a superior hunting dog and it is a known fact that dogs like him can see the paranormal.

He will warn us if Wanda comes floating around during the night.

After lots of fiddling and fussing and arguing with Ted and organising comics and books and torches and several quick snacks, it is time to get in our sleeping bags. But first, Gloria and I have to go outside … and visit the drop dunny.

Awesome refuses to come with us. He just sits in the middle of the sleeping circle and stares at Ted. But it is not because he likes Ted. It is because Ted has two party pies and a jam button under his pillow.

'Gloria,' I say as we pick our way over the moonlit ground, 'do you have any other secrets?'

Gloria stops and shines her torch on me for a second.

'What do you mean?' she says.

'Well, it's just that you didn't tell me you were in the Chosen Few and then you just turned up here tonight and I wondered …'

I pick up a rock and throw it into the bushes. A bird screeches and we flash our torches around.

'I couldn't say anything about the Chosen Few,' says

Gloria, walking on, 'because it's the biggest secret and you can't talk about the biggest secrets just anywhere. Besides, *you* didn't tell *me* about the Chosen Few.'

'Well, no,' I say. 'I didn't.'

'Well, there you go then,' says Gloria, grinning in the moonlight. 'We're even.'

And it's true. We are even. And that's when I decide that secrets are the most complicated things in the whole world. And I also decide not to ask Gloria if she has any secret best friends who are away on holidays. Sometimes you just have to know when to stop worrying.

We walk on a bit further.

'Tan,' whispers Gloria, and she digs inside her pocket. 'There is one more thing ...'

Oh no. Just when I thought everything was settled.

Gloria stops and holds out her hand. 'I've got something for you,' she says quietly.

I shine the torch on her hand.

'I hope you like it,' says Gloria.

I stop dead in my tracks. It is the most beautiful TAN necklace I have ever seen. It has special glass beads either side of my name and the whole thing glitters like a rare jewel.

'It is a work of art, Gloria,' I whisper as I tie the necklace around my neck. 'An absolute work of art.'

'It's waterproof, too,' says Gloria.

'Then I will never take it off,' I say, patting the necklace. 'Never, ever.'

And even though it is dark, I know that we are both grinning.

14

The drop dunny is way down the back of Purple Haunt, at the edge of the clearing. Beyond it are tangled black trees and bushes as far as you can see. Even the moonlight cannot shine into it. It is my sincere hope there are no wild animals lurking in there. Especially no emus.

'You go first,' I say. 'You've had more Fanta than me.'

'All right,' says Gloria, looking around. 'You stand guard.'

I flash my torch about while Gloria is in the drop dunny. I am keeping an eye out for strange disturbances. I am also keeping an eye out for Wandering Wanda. It would be awful for Gloria to be trapped in a drop dunny by an angry ghost. I have my torch in one hand and my water pistol in the other. It is loaded with creek water. It could be just enough to distract Wanda if we need to make a quick escape.

There is a rustle in the bush. I swing around. 'Who's there?' I say, pointing my water pistol. 'I'm armed, you know.'

'What?' says Gloria, from inside the drop dunny.

'Nothing,' I say. I lower my water pistol. I do not want to

alarm Gloria. But I am feeling extremely wary. I am sure I heard something ... menacing. I stare into the bush, but it is hopeless. I can't see a thing.

'Pew!' says Gloria, staggering out of the drop dunny. She is fumbling with the cord on her cargo pants. 'I'm glad that's over. It stinks in there.'

'Shh!' I say.

'What?' whispers Gloria, moving closer.

'I heard something,' I mutter.

There is more rustling in the bush.

'There it is again,' I whisper.

'Who's there?' says Gloria loudly. She shines her torch around, but I push it down.

'Shh,' I say. 'Keep your torch down. Whatever it is, I think it's coming for the light.'

Gloria's eyes widen and she opens her mouth, but it's too late. There is a flurry of snapping branches and all at once something fast and shadowy darts out of the bush and straight across our path.

'What is it?' gasps Gloria as we back up against the drop dunny.

'I ... I don't know,' I squeak.

We are rooted to the spot. The dim outline of 'the thing' skulks in the shadows. Its shining eyes bore into us.

'*Shoo!*' says Gloria, and she stamps her foot. The creature crouches lower and the darkness closes around it. Now we can't see it at all. But it's still there.

I can hear my own heart pounding ... or maybe it's Gloria's.

'Should we run?' whispers Gloria.

'No way,' I say. 'It might chase us. I've got a better idea.'

I raise my water pistol. I take aim at the bush.

'Get away, you *thing!*' I scream, and I squeeze the trigger.

Nothing happens. The water pistol is jammed. I shake it and whack it and shake it again.

'Come *on*,' I say under my breath.

'Squeeze harder,' cries Gloria, jiggling up and down. 'Squeeze harder!'

I take aim again, close my eyes, and squeeze with all my might. 'Take that!' I yell, and I squeeze so hard the trigger snaps and the stopper pops and a jet of muddy creek water shoots out and squirts us both in the face.

'Argh!' we both scream together. 'Run!'

I throw the water pistol in the air and we take off. We have no idea whether the creature is chasing us. We run faster than we have ever run in our lives and we do not look back – not even for a nanosecond.

When we get back to Purple Haunt, everyone is on the veranda. Awesome is barking and wagging his tail. Amber is clutching Doodad, and Jem is clutching Amber. Ted is laughing and Rose is holding up the red candle and peering into the night. Emerald is standing at the top of the steps with her hands on her hips.

'You idiots,' she says. 'What was all that screaming about? The entire valley must have heard you.'

Gloria and I throw ourselves up the steps.

'It was *horrible* …' I gasp.

'It was huge … and black … and it leapt out of the bush!' pants Gloria.

'Sweet,' says Rose, holding up the candle. 'It sounds wicked.'

'Oh, it was, Rose,' I say, 'it was. It had evil yellow eyes … and pointy fangs.'

'It was staring straight at us,' says Gloria.

'No, it wasn't just staring at us,' I say, turning to Emerald. 'It was *hunting* us!' I wipe my wet face on my sleeve.

'Whatever,' says Emerald, leaning back against the railing.

'Yeah, right,' says Ted, throwing a stone into the night. 'It was a fox, you dorks. That's all it was.'

'A fox?' says Gloria. 'No way! I've seen plenty of foxes. This was too big. Too bold. Too—'

'It *was* a fox,' says Emerald. 'I saw it myself. It ran past here a second ago, clear as day.'

'Probably sniffing around for party pies,' says Ted, and he thinks he is hilarious.

'Hush,' snaps Jem, and she takes Doodad from Amber and tucks the silly dog under her arm. 'The Chosen Few do not treat each other so rudely. Come inside, Tan and Gloria. It is time you rested and tidied yourselves up. You both look frightful. Ted. Make yourself useful. There's plenty of milk in the Esky. You can make everyone a chocolate milk.'

'With crushed Maltesers on top?' says Amber.

'Of course,' says Jem, stroking Doodad's ears. 'And from now on if anyone wants to use the outhouse, Awesome is to go with them.'

Awesome looks at Jem and pricks up his ears. Jem gives him a nod. Then she spins around and marches inside.

It is an unexpected thing, but Jem is very good at being the boss.

Gloria and I spend the rest of the night talking and giggling and telling our story again and again until eventually the others fall asleep.

For a while, we listen to them snore and scratch, then Gloria opens her book and puffs up her pillow.

'Tan,' she says, lying back, 'where did you get that water pistol?'

'It was in a Christmas stocking,' I say, rolling over.

'Do you think it's any good?' says Gloria, yawning.

'No,' I say. 'It is not. It is a very poor-quality water pistol and I am going to write to the Christmas stocking people as soon as I get home.'

'Good plan,' says Gloria. And the next second her book slides to the floor and Gloria is snoring.

I am glad we have stopped talking about water and water pistols. I never did get to use the drop dunny.

Dear Diary

I am writing to you by the light of Amber's Pretty Princess torch — you know, the one with the coloured glitter in its lens. I would rather use Amber's batteries than mine, even though her torch is embarrassing.

Gloria thinks the drop dunny creature was a puma. There are not supposed to be pumas in this country.
But Gloria said there are old people who say there are some escaped ones living in the bush. I did not know anything about this, but I am sure it is true.

I have a devised a theory about Wandering Wanda.
I told Gloria and she agrees with me. We will tell everyone in the morning.

It is an exciting thing to be in the Chosen Few.

Truly
Tan

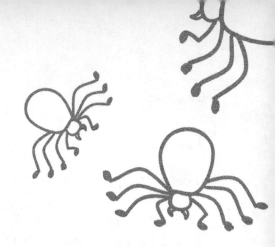

Episode Eight:

Spiders, Sketchbooks

and the Ghost Gum Grave

15

Awesome is in the drawing room doorway. He is jumping around and barking. Emerald is beside him. 'OMG,' she is saying. 'OMG.'

This is mobile-phone talk for Oh My God. Emerald was the first one up this morning, but now we are all awake and we are standing beside her in Purple Haunt and looking shocked.

All the Barbie dolls have fallen off the shelves. One of them even has its hands in the air, and its hair is sticking up as if it got the biggest fright. I am sure it did not look like that last night. There are also hundreds and thousands AND cornflakes all over the floor. And the clay caveman's head has rolled off the shelf and landed in a box of Cheezels.

'The letterbox!' says Ted, and he dashes out.

I run my detective eyes along the shelves. Everything else is exactly as we left it and I am grateful the black-eyed brain-boiler is still in its jar. Everyone is going crazy, but Gloria and I stay calm and businesslike, because we have a theory.

'The letterbox is over again!' yells Ted, and we run out to

the veranda. Sure enough the letterbox has fallen over … or been pushed over.

'Quick,' says Jem, 'get that magical camera. We need hard evidence of these happenings.'

But Jem is too late. Rose is already leaping down the steps with her box brownie.

No one is keeping an eye on Doodad. 'Doodad, no!' shouts Amber, and she runs back into the drawing room.

Doodad is sniffing at the mess and running about wagging her tail. She looks up. There are hundreds and thousands all over her snout.

'Oh, dear,' says Amber, scooping up Doodad and brushing her face. 'I hope the ghost hasn't poisoned the hundreds and thousands.'

Doodad sneezes.

'Don't worry, Amber,' I say, leaning against the doorframe. 'This is not the work of a vengeful ghost.'

'No,' says Gloria, joining me. 'That's right. We are dealing with a *frustrated* ghost. Not a mean ghost.'

'Right,' says Emerald, coming between us. 'And you know this because …?'

I put my hands on my hips and turn to face Emerald.

Sometimes you really have to spell things out for Emerald. But before I can get started, Gloria grabs my arm.

'Come on,' she says quickly, and she leads me over to the Eskies. 'Let's get some food and have breakfast by the creek. Then we can tell everyone our theory.'

Emerald puts on her big round sunglasses and heads down the steps. 'I can hardly wait,' she says. But I don't think she means it.

'Any more watermelon?' says Amber.

'Here,' says Emerald, and she passes her a big chunk.

It was a good idea to have breakfast down here. We have laid the picnic rug under the ghost gum. We have watermelon, rockmelon, nectarines, cherries, strawberries, grapes, cinnamon teacake and a few leftover Maltesers.

Ted throws a stick and Awesome plunges into the creek after it. Awesome does not like fruit and he does not know that we have a cake, so he is ignoring us. The hot sun is blinking through the branches of the ghost gum and I notice Gloria is wearing her army camouflage hat. I will have to put mine on soon, too.

'Okay,' says Emerald, spitting watermelon seeds in the dirt. 'Tell us your theory, you two.'

'Yes,' says Jem, who is trying to peel a grape. 'Please share your theory with us. I'm sure it will be riveting.'

'Okay,' I say, getting up and balancing on a tree root. 'It's like this. Gloria and I talked about it all night and we think Wanda is trying to tell us something.'

'This ghost isn't doing mean things,' says Gloria, standing beside me and pointing a piece of rockmelon skin at everyone. 'But she is trying to get our attention.'

'There's something she's not happy about,' I add. 'And that's why she keeps pushing the letterbox over and spilling stuff on the floor and—'

'And she won't rest until we put everything right,' says a voice from above. It's Rose. She is in the tree.

'That's right,' I say, looking up at Rose. She looks like a scraggy black crow, but I would never tell her that.

'It's like I said before – why would Wanda haunt Purple Haunt?' I say, looking around at everyone.

'What are her *motives*?' says Ted, in a silly singsong voice. He bites into a nectarine. 'Yeah, yeah. You said all that before, Tan,' he says, but he can't talk properly, because there is juice running down his chin and he has to slurp it up.

'Jem,' I say, ignoring Ted's bad manners, 'how far is Wanda's shack from here?'

'Not far,' says Jem. 'It's just over the creek and across a few paddocks.'

'Well, I think we need to investigate,' I say.

'So do I,' says Gloria. 'There has to be something in that old shack. Something that will give us a clue about Wandering Wanda and why she's bothering us.'

'Brilliant!' says Rose, and she drops out of the tree and lands softly like a big bat. 'Let's check it out right now. If Purple Haunt is haunted, imagine what the old shack's like.'

'I am imagining,' says Amber, turning pale. 'I am imagining.'

We pack up the breakfast stuff. Then we grab our hats and backpacks and water bottles, and Rose gets her box brownie and Amber gets her Pretty Princess torch and Jem gets her

Pretty Princess bangles and Emerald cracks it because she has forgotten her lip gloss. Then we head off for Wanda's shack.

'Just a minute,' I say as we are leaving, and I run back into Purple Haunt.

I almost forgot my Spy 'n' Pry magnifying glass. It would be unprofessional to go investigating without it.

'I don't know what we'll find when we get there,' says Jem as we make our way across the paddocks. 'Mum and some other old ladies cleaned up Wanda's shack after she died. Mum was utterly exhausted. She said Wanda's shack was a complete shemozzle.'

'Yeah,' says Ted. 'They took three ute-loads of junk to the tip.'

'Oh, well,' I say. 'You never know.'

'That's right,' says Gloria, tucking her hair up under her hat. 'You never know what you might find if you look hard enough.'

Ted jogs ahead. He has a tennis ball and he is playing fetch with Awesome. But Awesome is getting sick of it. He has a droopy, bored look on his face. Plus, he is annoyed with Doodad. She tried to fetch the ball a couple of times and she tripped him up. Doodad is always under someone's feet.

'Are you sure this isn't illegal?' says Amber as she hurries along beside us. 'I mean, shouldn't we have a search warrant or something?'

'No, no,' says Jem. 'We've all lived on this land for years. The neighbours won't mind if we take a peek in the old shack. We're almost family.'

'Well, I still think it's creepy,' says Amber, 'sneaking around in a dead person's shack.'

'Oh, Amber,' says Jem, admiring her Pretty Princess bangles. 'You mustn't let your imagination run away with you. What could possibly go wrong?'

We walk on for a bit then suddenly Rose stops. 'There it is!' she says.

A tin roof shines through the trees. We can also see a couple of water tanks and a rusty red truck with no wheels.

'Yes, that's it,' says Jem.

Rose lines up her box brownie and while we are waiting I notice it is very quiet out here in the middle of nowhere. It is also very still. And the old shack looks especially quiet and especially still and especially ... shimmery.

'There's a strange feeling in the air,' mutters Rose as she peers down the lens of her box brownie.

'What do you mean?' says Emerald.

But I know exactly what Rose means. There *is* a strange feeling in the air and I can sense the strange feeling and it feels very ... **eerie.**

None of us move for a minute. Even Ted has stopped in his tracks. So have Awesome and Doodad.

Emerald gets impatient. 'Well, what are we waiting for?' she says. 'Let's get this over with.'

Emerald stomps off toward the shack. We all stare after her.

'Do you think she'll go in?' whispers Jem.

'She'd have to be crazy,' whispers Amber.

'Why are we whispering?' whispers Gloria.

'I don't know,' I whisper.

'What?' whispers Amber.

'Shush!' whispers Rose.

It is an odd thing, but people often whisper when there is a strange feeling in the air.

When we get to the shack, Ted has gone around the back and Emerald is waiting on the porch.

'Took your time,' she says as we join her. She nods her head at the front door. 'You go first, Rose,' she says. 'You're the paranormal expert.'

The door is made of old planks that are grey and splintery. It has a rusty ring for a handle and no lock. A horseshoe is nailed to it. A pair of gumboots stand beside the door and a woolly black shawl hangs from a hook. Rose pushes the shawl to one side. There is a sign behind it. It says:

KEEP OUT!

'See,' whispers Amber. 'We're supposed to keep out!'

'Not any more,' says Jem. 'Wanda's dead. And you forget, Amber, we are trying to help her.'

'Whatever,' says Emerald. 'Are we going in or not?'

'Move aside,' says Rose, and she hangs her box brownie around her neck and pushes past.

The heavy door creaks as she turns the handle, but it only opens a fraction. Rose gives it another push and carefully pokes her head inside. We all gather behind her.

'Hello?' calls Rose. 'Anybody home?'

Emerald stamps her foot. 'Of course there's nobody home,' she says. 'She's *dead*! Just go in, Rose. You're blocking the doorway.'

'Okay, okay,' says Rose, and she squeezes through the crack and disappears inside. But Emerald does not follow. In fact, none of us follow. We just stand there.

I look around. The porch of Wanda's shack is made of stony bricks pushed into the dirt and it is higgledy-piggledy. There are lots of bushes with pink and blue flowers growing around the porch and this is surprising. I did not think Wanda would like flowers. There is also a huge swan statue out in the middle of the front yard. The swan has been made out of a tractor tyre and painted white and I think it is very attractive. It has piles of marigolds growing in its back. Just as well QV is not here. She would go crazy for those marigolds.

At the end of the porch, there is the biggest rose bush I have ever seen. It is covered in deep-red roses and there are bees buzzing around it. It is tangled and twisted and has thorns like rhino horns. It is a creepy rose bush. But it smells nice.

'Come on,' calls Rose. 'Come inside. It's cool!'

We all look at each other. Ted is over at the old truck. He has the bonnet up and he's looking underneath. Ted is poking things and rattling things and I can tell he thinks he knows everything about trucks. Awesome is up on the tray at the back, sniffing around. And Doodad is under the truck doing a wee. Doodad is so … inappropriate.

INAPPROPRIATE: this is when you say or do the wrong thing at the wrong time. I only know this word because of Miss Dragone. On my first day at school she said my cat skeleton was inappropriate. Another time, when I asked her if she thought Mr Lamble was handsome, she said I was inappropriate. I'm not sure why.

'Boys are such cowards,' says Jem. 'Come on. Let's go inside.'

Jem gives the door another nudge and it swings wide open. She takes Amber's hand and slowly they inch their way into the dark, dark shack. I am not sure if Amber is still breathing.

Gloria and I are next, but we are feeling a bit … eerie. The KEEP OUT sign is watching us. It feels like there are big googly eyes behind it. If we go in, what will we find? What lurky things lurk in a dead person's shack? Will the ghost leap out of a cupboard and grab us by the hair and hurl us out the door and chase us into the bush? These are the things I am thinking and I am sure Gloria is thinking them, too.

Emerald is craning over my shoulder and trying to see inside. She looks like a blowfly in those silly sunglasses.

'You will have to take off those sunglasses,' I say over my shoulder. 'Or you'll crash into something and break your neck.'

Emerald gives me a shove and I stumble through the door. Gloria is right behind me, giggling.

'Shush!' says Jem as we fall inside, but Gloria keeps giggling.

'Sorry,' she sputters. 'I always giggle when I'm nervous.'

It is dark and gloomy inside Wanda's shack – a lot like a ghost house you would see at the Show. I hope there are no men in skeleton suits hiding in the corners.

'It's only got two rooms,' says Rose, appearing out of the darkness.

Gloria and I stand there, blinking. Emerald's sunglasses are on her head now, and Amber is standing next to Jem, tapping at her Pretty Princess torch.

'There's something wrong with this torch,' says Amber, looking down the lens.

'The batteries are flat,' says Rose.

'But they're only new,' says Amber, giving the torch a shake.

'I told you not to buy that Pretty Princess brand,' I say, looking at the ceiling. 'It's very dodgy stuff.'

'It is not,' starts Amber. 'It's—'

'Hold on,' says Rose.

A piece of heavy green velvet is nailed over the window. Rose tucks back the velvet and the sun shines through. It lights up the cobwebs and dead flies that are dangling in the window, but at least we can see.

The room we are in must have been the kitchen. But there is not much in here.

On the far wall there is a wood stove with a black kettle sitting on it. Two cooking pots and a couple of blue-and-white tin mugs hang from nails above it. There is a sagging brown armchair beside the stove. It has bits of stuffing sticking out of the arms and a big dent in the seat.

'That's where Wanda used to sit,' I whisper.

'Creepy,' says Gloria.

There is a small table with battered metal legs and a faded pattern of yellow roses.

'That's where Wanda used to eat,' says Gloria.

'Creepy,' I say.

'Shush, you two,' says Amber.

'Yeah, give it a rest,' says Emerald, and she tugs on the door of a tall cupboard.

We all stop still. That cupboard is just the right size for a skeleton ... or an angry ghost.

'I wouldn't touch that cupboard if I were you, Emerald,' I warn. 'That cupboard is highly suspicious.'

'Sure, Tan,' says Emerald, and she yanks the doorknob.

The cupboard jolts, the door flies open and a huge fishing net drops on Emerald's head. We all scream. Even Rose.

'Get it off me!' squeals Emerald, and she flails around like a snared squid. But the more she flails, the more tangled she gets.

'Hold still,' says Rose. 'I can't get it off if you keep jumping around.'

Emerald groans, but she stops wriggling.

'Pew,' says Jem as she tries to help. 'This net smells like dead fish.'

'Just get it off me!' cries Emerald again.

'All right, all right,' says Jem. 'But you must hold still, silly billy!'

Emerald glares at Jem through the fishing net. Emerald has never, ever been called 'silly billy'.

'I hate this place,' whines Amber as she untangles Emerald's bent sunglasses from the net. 'And this is a useless investigation. There's nothing here to help us. Not a thing. I think we should get out right now.'

'No way,' says Rose. 'We can't give up yet. Remember, we're here to help Wanda.'

Rose gives the net a firm tug and Emerald bursts free. Her hair is everywhere and she looks wild-eyed and hostile. She is sniffing at her clothes and hands.

'What are you two looking at?' she growls, but Gloria and I are not looking at Emerald. We are looking at the ceiling – and trying not to laugh.

Rose bundles up the net and puts it in Emerald's arms. 'Come on. Let's check out the bedroom,' says Rose. 'It's bound to be full of secrets.'

'Yes,' says Jem. 'Come along, Chosen Few. We must rally!'

'Two minutes,' hisses Emerald as she places the fishing net back in the cupboard. 'Two minutes and I'm out of here.'

It is my guess Emerald won't be opening any more suspicious cupboards today.

16

Wanda's bedroom is even quieter than the rest of the shack. It's dark, too. For a moment we stand in the doorway and listen – although I don't know what we are listening for.

There is an iron bed in the middle of the room, but it's just a frame. There's no mattress or pillows or blankets. Not even a sleeping bag. Everything has been cleared out.

'Now, that bed is definitely creepy,' whispers Gloria, and I agree. The empty bed is definitely … unsettling.

We have all gone quiet. It feels like there is an invisible barrier across the doorway. Then Rose gasps. 'Look at the walls!' And she steps straight through the invisible barrier. Emerald follows.

The walls of Wanda's bedroom are totally covered in newspaper clippings and magazine pages and old black-and-white photos and ancient movie posters.

'Look – dancers!' says Amber, and she runs into the room. Jem runs after her.

Now there is only Gloria and me left on the other side of the invisible barrier. Gloria and I are much more skilled investigators. That is why we are so ... wary.

We can see there are ballerinas and tap dancers and ladies doing the cancan among Wanda's clippings. Of course, that is the only reason Amber got so brave and went in.

'Wanda must have been a dancer,' says Jem as she examines the pictures.

'Or a pilot,' says Amber. 'There're loads of old planes in these pictures.'

'I wonder if that's her on that camel?' says Rose thoughtfully.

'Right,' says Emerald, looking over Rose's shoulder. 'So Wanda was a dancing, aeroplane-flying camel-rider. Great investigation, guys. That should explain why she's haunting Purple Haunt.'

It is time for me and Gloria to take a look. The Chosen Few are getting confused.

'Look at this, Tan,' says Gloria as we go in. 'Do you think Wanda was a nurse?'

Gloria is pointing to a row of black-and-white photos. They show old fashioned nurses with big white veils and stiff aprons and stiff faces. I pull out my Spy 'n' Pry magnifying glass. Below the photos it says:

London, 1943.

'Wow,' says Rose, coming over. 'Wanda must have been in World War Two. She must have been ancient when she died.'

It is like being in an art gallery, here in Wanda's room – except this is an interesting art gallery and we are not bored out of our brains. Not one little bit.

'Check out all the books,' I say.

There are rows of books, stacked neatly below the window. There are magazines, too, and piles of old newspapers. Gloria and I kneel down to look.

'Do you think Wanda would mind if we took a peek?' says Gloria. 'I love old books.'

'I don't think she'd mind,' I say, gently turning a cover. 'So long as we're careful.'

There are books about birds and books about dogs and horses and reptiles and native animals. There are gardening books and books about London and books about the Queen of England, who I think lives in a tower somewhere near London Bridge (but I could be wrong). There are also books about machines and motorbikes and boats.

'Wow,' says Gloria. 'Wanda liked reading, didn't she?'

'Yes,' says Jem. 'Mum mentioned the books. She said they're all going to charity. The magazines and newspapers are going to the recycling mill.'

By now, we are all on the floor. Amber is pouring over ancient fashion magazines and Jem joins her. They start giggling. The rest of us are flicking through the books – even Emerald. Then Rose pulls out a yellowed newspaper and starts reading our horoscopes. Mine is especially good. It says my talents are rare and will soon earn me great respect. I like the idea of that.

Then Rose gets to Amber's horoscope. 'Pisces, beware,' says Rose quietly, and Amber stops giggling. 'The full moon brings dark tidings and dangerous, ghostly disturbances.'

'Give me that!' says Amber, and she tries to grab the newspaper. 'You're making that up.'

Rose laughs and waves the paper in the air.

'Stop it,' says Emerald. 'These were Wanda's things. You have to be careful. Even if it is just for recycling.'

Amber and Rose look guilty. They quickly tidy their piles.

'Hey, look at this,' I say, easing some magazines aside. 'There's a sketchbook under these.'

The sketchbook has black material on the cover and a dirty red ribbon down the spine. Everyone leans over to get a better look. I slowly open the cover – and a huge spider falls out and runs across my knee. We all scream and everyone starts whacking my knee and I start yelling and then there's a loud bang at the window.

We look up. There is a figure at the window. It is draped in a woolly black shawl and swaying back and forth. 'Be gone. Be gone. Be gone,' it moans. 'Be gone or I will hang you from the ghost gum …'

We all sit frozen in horror. The figure raises its blackened hands and scratches at the window. *Sccrick. Sccrick. Sccrick.*

'Argh!' We leap up. A stack of books collapses. A mouse darts across the room. We scramble for the door and everyone tries to squeeze through at once. But Amber is first out. We clamber after her and stumble through the dark kitchen. The tall cupboard lurches and a pile of walking sticks and brooms tumble out.

'It's a trap!' screams Amber as she trips on a broom handle.

'It's her!' screams Jem, and she leaps over Amber and wrenches open the front door. 'It's the ghost!'

We all fly out the door.

For a moment the bright sun blinds us. We stop by the swan statue and try to catch our breath.

'How wicked was that!' pants Roses, bending forward and gripping her sides.

'I think I'm going to be sick,' whimpers Amber, and Jem pats her arm.

'Don't worry, Amber,' she says. 'We're out in the sun now. Wanda can't get us here.' But Jem has gone white and she doesn't look too sure. None of us do.

'Shh,' says Emerald. 'What's that noise?'

'It sounds like someone *laughing*,' I say, and right at that moment Ted comes around the side of the house. He is wrapped in a black shawl and he is cracking up.

'You should have seen your faces!' says Ted, staggering about. 'You looked like stunned mullets.'

'Why you little—' says Emerald, and she charges at Ted. But he is too quick and Emerald is too wobbly to chase him.

'Be gone, be gone, *beeeee goooooone!*' yells Ted, from behind a tree. He roars laughing again.

Ted thinks he is the best comedian in town (and it is kind of funny when you think about it). But he will not be laughing when Emerald gets hold of him.

STUNNED MULLET: a mullet is a fish. A stunned mullet is a fish that has had the sense knocked out of it and its mouth is gaping and its eyes are popping out of its head and it looks stupid.

17

Jem flops to the ground and leans against the swan. We all join her. Rose sticks a marigold behind her ear. 'So much for our investigation,' she says. 'Did anyone get any clues?'

We all shrug.

'Well, wild horses couldn't get me back in that shack,' says Emerald. 'It's hideous.'

'But what about the sketchbook?' I say, and everyone looks at me.

'What about it?' says Emerald.

'We never got to examine it,' I say. 'It could contain vital evidence.'

'Poo!' says Amber. 'The sketchbook was probably full of recipes.'

'Or stamps,' says Jem.

'Well, I think it's important,' I say. 'And so does Gloria.'

'What?' says Gloria. She is digging in the dirt with a twig. 'Oh, yes. The sketchbook. Yes. It's definitely important.'

'Good,' I say, jumping up. 'Come on, Gloria. Let's go and get it.'

Everyone stares at us. Gloria stops digging and looks up at me. 'I can't, Tan,' she whispers. 'It's too scary.'

I am shocked. I never thought Gloria would give up. 'But, Gloria,' I say, 'we need that sketchbook. I know because I have a hunch and Great Detectives always follow their hunches.'

'I know,' says Gloria. 'I'm really sorry, Tan. It's just too freaky in there.'

Poor Gloria. She looks as miserable as Awesome on a bad day.

'It doesn't matter, Gloria,' I say quickly. 'You stay out here and back me up.'

'Okay,' says Gloria quietly. 'I'll be behind the swan if you need me.'

I turn to face the shack, but it does not look very inviting. It looks *loomy* and sinister and it makes my stomach go tight.

'I think ...' I whisper, 'maybe we should leave it for today. There are too many spiders and mice in that shack. It's not safe.'

'Yes,' says Gloria. 'That's a great idea. Let's leave it for today.

The place is crawling with spiders and rodents. We saw for ourselves.'

'That's right,' I say. 'Wanda's shack is definitely a health risk.'

Everyone nods and they all agree with me and this is an unusual feeling.

'Right. That's settled,' says Emerald, putting on her crooked sunglasses. 'Let's get out of here.'

But just as we are getting up, Amber says, 'Has anyone seen Doodad?'

We all look around. Awesome is over in the trees with Ted, but Doodad is nowhere to be seen.

'Oh, no!' says Amber. 'I hope she's not lost in the bush. We'll never find her alive. She's too little. Too delicate—'

'Too stupid,' I say as the tip of Doodad's tail disappears inside Wanda's shack.

'Doodad!' screams Amber. 'Doodad, come here!'

But Doodad does not come. Even if she knew her name, she still wouldn't come. Doodad has a head full of air. She always does exactly what she pleases.

'No,' groans Amber. 'What if she gets trapped? What if Wanda whacks her with a walking stick ... or locks her in that evil cupboard? Someone's got to save her!'

'You go,' says Emerald. 'She's your dog!'

'I can't go in there again,' whispers Amber. 'I just can't. What about you, Rose? You're brave.'

But Rose crosses her arms.

And now Amber starts to cry.

Everyone goes red and it is a very embarrassing thing to be standing around a marigold swan while your sister is crying.

'For goodness sake,' I say. 'I'll go. I'll get your stupid dog.'

'Thanks, Tan,' sniffs Amber, and she wipes a trail of watery snot on her sleeve. It is my observation that people often forget their manners when they are crying. Even prissy people like Amber.

I march back to the shack. I am not letting a spindly spider and a smarty-pants boy in a black shawl scare me. The Chosen Few stare after me. Even Ted is watching from the trees.

'Hey,' I yell from the porch, 'someone better put that shawl back … or Ted will be the one who's hanging from the ghost gum.'

Jem nods and signals to Ted to get moving.

It is fun being the brave one, and the bossy one, and the paranormal expert. As I open the creaky door, these thoughts make me feel quite ... daring.

18

Exactly sixty seconds later I step out of the shack and back into the sunny morning. I concentrate hard. I am trying to walk calmly, not run like a mad thing. It would not be dignified for a paranormal expert to come screaming out of a deserted shack. Especially not a paranormal expert who also has the mind of a Great Detective.

I have Doodad under one arm and the sketchbook under the other. I also have Amber's *Pretty Princess* torch in my back pocket. It was right where it landed when she screamed and threw it in the air.

Everyone claps as I walk across the prickly grass to the marigold swan, even Ted. My mission has been an overwhelming success. I am a hero. Gloria gives me a hug and Rose slaps me on the back.

'Oh, Tan!' says Amber, taking Doodad from me. 'Thank you. Thank you.'

Doodad has on her usual ninny-dog grin. She has no idea of the danger she was in.

'You got the sketchbook,' says Rose. 'Sweet.'

'Yes, Rose,' I say. 'It is sweet and I think we should sit down straight away and check it out.'

'Absolutely,' says Emerald.

'What's in it?' says Ted, sidling up.

'We don't know, Ted,' I say, holding the sketchbook close to my chest. 'But we are sure it holds vital clues.'

'We can sit under that gum tree with Awesome if you like,' says Ted, adjusting his hat. 'It's away from the shack and there's plenty of grass under it.'

'Thank you, Ted,' I say. 'That would be very nice.'

Ted nods and puts his hands in his pockets. It seems that even Ted has nice manners when he is curious.

We settle under the tree and I give the sketchbook a shake. No spiders fall out. Awesome sniffs it and yawns. I slowly open the cover and turn back the onion paper.

'Wow!' say Gloria and Emerald together.

The sketchbook is full of drawings of gum trees and cockatoos and echidnas and wild flowers. There is even one of the old truck.

'They're delightful,' says Jem, shading her eyes.

I keep turning the pages.

'Look at all these fox drawings,' I say. Awesome leans against me as if he is trying to see.

'There are stacks of them,' says Ted, breathing down my neck. 'Page after page.'

I get out my Spy 'n' Pry magnifying glass and hold it over the fox drawings.

'Does anyone notice anything?' I say to the others.

'Wanda liked foxes?' says Amber.

'Yes, Amber. Wanda liked foxes,' I say. 'But do you notice anything else?'

'They're really good?' says Emerald.

'Yes, Emerald. We've already said that,' I say. 'But there's something else. Look closely.'

Gloria examines the fox pictures, but even she doesn't notice the vital clue.

'It is the *same fox* in every picture,' I say finally.

'How do you know that?' says Ted, squinting at the pictures.

'Because, Ted,' I say, 'look closely and you will see that this fox, the fox that is in all the sketches, always has half its left ear missing.'

'Oh my God,' whispers Rose. She knows exactly what I am about to say.

'You know what this means?' I look around at the rest of the Chosen Few. But they look … vacant.

'It means,' I say, pushing Awesome's head away, 'that this sketchbook fox and the *dead fence-post fox* are the same fox!'

'What?' says Ted.

'You're kidding,' says Emerald, and she takes the sketchbook from me. She stares at the pictures.

'The dead fence-post fox must have been Wanda's pet,' says Rose under her breath.

'Exactly,' I say.

'Oh, dear,' cries Amber, and she hugs Doodad. 'Poor, poor Wanda! That real estate agent took her darling pet fox and used it as a *road sign*!'

'That's right,' I say.

Jem covers her mouth. She is horrified.

'Then I threw it over Purple Haunt's letterbox and used it as a mascot,' says Ted flatly. Jem glares at him. 'I didn't know!' he says. 'I didn't have a clue that grungy old fox was someone's pet. I just thought it was, you know, feral.'

Gloria and I exchange looks. This is all significant information and we know it. This sketchbook is what we would call `Exhibit A`.

'Ted,' I say, twirling my magnifying glass. 'Where did you bury the dead fox?'

'Oh, you know,' says Ted. 'Around.' He scrapes at his shoe with a stone.

'Around where exactly?' says Gloria.

'Just around,' says Ted, and he throws the stone in the bush.

'Excuse me, Ted,' says Jem briskly. 'A proper answer, please. This is important.'

Ted fiddles with his shoe a bit more. 'I didn't,' he says finally.

'What do you mean?' says Jem, pushing up her bangles.

'I mean, I didn't bury it,' says Ted, glaring at Jem. 'It was too hot and I couldn't be bothered digging a hole, so I just chucked it.'

'WHAT?' yells Jem.

'It's all right, Jem,' says Amber, patting Jem's arm. 'He didn't mean any harm. He's just a *boy*.'

'I put the dead fox in a hessian bag,' says Ted quickly. 'Then I tied up the bag and chucked it in a hollow tree.'

'A hollow tree!' says Rose. 'Don't you get it, Ted?'

I don't know why, but right at this moment I feel a bit sorry for Ted. He looks like a cornered possum who has been cornered while raiding someone's world-class tree house. And I would know about these things.

'Of course Ted gets it,' I say, and Ted looks grateful that I have saved him from Rose. 'The unburied fox is the reason why Wanda is haunting Purple Haunt. In fact,' I add thoughtfully, 'it was probably the dead fox's ghost that chased us down at the drop dunny.'

There are gasps all round. Even Ted looks shocked.

'That fox must have a proper burial,' says Rose, 'or Wanda will never ever rest. She will wander and haunt forever.'

'I've read about this kind of thing,' whispers Gloria as she takes the sketchbook from Emerald and gently closes the cover.

'Of course you have, Gloria,' I say. 'This kind of thing is a common ectoplasmic problem.'

'Well then,' says Amber, jumping up and throwing Doodad over her shoulder. 'To the dead fox, Ted, and make it quick. That fox was Wanda's pet and it deserves a proper funeral. It is up to us to put things right.'

I have never, ever seen Amber act so … normal.

We follow Ted here and there and around and about until at last he finds the hollow tree with the hessian bag in it. It is a very sorry sight (and very stinky). Amber has to look away while Ted jiggles the bag to get it out.

Then we have a big debate about where to bury the dead fox. Emerald says back at the shack, but none of us want to go back there. Then Ted says under the ghost gum down by the creek would be the best place, because that is where he found the sticks in the W shape and he thinks that this was an *omen*. Rose says this is a very insightful thing to say and

Ted goes red. I'm not sure what 'insightful' means, but it must be good, because I can tell Ted is pleased with himself.

So, in the end, we bury the dead fox under the ghost gum. Ted digs a big hole and Awesome helps him. Amber names the fox 'Lopsy Fox' because of its lopsided ears and Emerald hammers a sign on the tree that says, LOPSY FOX RIP.

Rose conducts the ceremony and Ted lowers the hessian bag into the hole. Then we all put a rock on the grave and I read out a poem.

POEM FOR LOPSY FOX

Beneath these rocks lies Lopsy Fox

Wanda's friend until the end
But then he had to go and die
with no one there to say goodbye

But now we're here
so have no fear

we won't forget you

Lopsy Fox.

It is a very moving moment and Amber and Jem start to cry. Then Rose says, 'The curse of the dead fox has now been lifted,' and Gloria scatters marigold petals on the grave and Emerald says, 'Wanda and Lopsy, may you both now rest in peace,' and Ted says 'Amen,' and that is the end of that.

```
OMEN: an omen is a sign. There were lots of
bad omens hanging around Purple Haunt while
Wanda was doing her haunting. All these omens
were signs that Wanda was not a happy ghost.
Paranormal experts must always learn to read
omens. It is a valuable skill and it is lucky
I have it.
```

19

It is Sunday night. Mum and Dad are outside on the love swing. They said they were glad to have us home and they missed us and it was very quiet without us. Then they went outside.

The lollipops and I are in the lounge room. Emerald has the whole couch to herself. She is cutting out pictures from her *Cosmo* magazines and gluing them in a fancy scrapbook. She is making a book called *Teenage Fashion Through the Ages*. It is a project for school. Emerald says there are many important projects you must do in year eight and we better not get in her way and we better not let any animals on the couch – especially Awesome, because he once swallowed a glue stick. Emerald thinks she is a famous fashion writer, but really she is just cutting and pasting and I did that in grade one.

Rose is on the floor. She is surrounded by bits of black lace and black ribbon and black satin and she is making a funeral outfit for one of her dolls. Rose said she was inspired and moved by Lopsy Fox's funeral and she will be wearing black all next week.

Amber is on the floor, too, but she is on the other side of the room. She is teaching Doodad to walk on her front legs. But they are having limited success. Doodad keeps tipping over – and so does Amber. Amber cannot believe her dog does not have hidden talents. But it has always been clear to me.

I am in the lounge room, too. I am sitting at the little writing desk under the window. QV and Awesome are snoozing at my feet. Babbles is on my shoulder. E is outside on the veranda. He is chasing giant moths. Every now and then he pops up at the window and hisses. He looks like a vampire cat and I jump and Babbles screeches. E is a very spiteful animal.

It is lucky I can ignore E, because I am working on an important assignment. It is my report on Wandering Wanda. It is my first report in the **Paranormal Ectoplasmic** section of my Secret Spy Files. This is what I have written so far:

✳ A GHOST AT REST ✳

The haunting of Purple Haunt was a curious
affair. In fact, some might say that PH was
not haunted at all. They would say there is
a logical explanation for all the paranormal
activity observed by myself and the Chosen Few.
Perhaps the letterbox kept falling over because
it was dodgy. Perhaps the mess in the drawing
room was caused by a trickster possum or an
ill-behaved fox ... or uneven shelving. Perhaps
the mysterious creature at the drop dunny was
just another fox, and the ectoplasmic image on
the photograph was actually a smudge and not
Wanda at all. And perhaps poor Lopsy Fox was
not cursed, but was simply the innocent
victim of sneaky local real estate agent
and champion hunter, Mr Barry Crisp.

Because I have the mind of a Great Detective
and because I am also a paranormal expert,
I have considered all these arguments. I have
thought about the evidence. I have weighed up
the clues. I have spoken closely with my fellow
investigator, Gloria Pappos. And I have read
the omens.

My conclusion? Purple Haunt was definitely
haunted. How do I know? Because there is no
explanation for the feathers up the skull's
nose, and sticks never, ever fall in the shape
of the letter 'W'.

Verdict? Haunting complete. Ghost at rest.
Case closed.

Dear Diary

I am writing to you by the light of my flashing prawn lamp — you know, the one with the blinking eyes and orange tail-lights. I have opened a new file in my Secret Spy Files. It is the Mystery of Purple Haunt. It is extremely Top Secret. Rose gave me a photo of Purple Haunt to stick on the cover. It looks mysteriously intriguing.

Mrs Murphy (who is Jem and Ted's mum) said Wanda's sketchbook was 'divine'. She said it was lucky we found it or it would have ended up as computer paper. Then Mrs Murphy rang the local history people. They said the sketchbook was an 'artefact' and they will keep it forever in a special glass case. They also said Wanda's shack is an important piece of history and although they cannot put it in a glass case, it will never be sold or pulled down and important people (such as Mr Lamble and the local mayor) will visit it. Mrs Murphy said she was thankful the shack was tidy.

Gloria will be coming to stay next weekend. We will sleep on mattresses in sleeping bags on the veranda and Gloria will bring her telescope and a good-quality water pistol.

I am not sure if I have found popularness since we moved to the country. But I have found Gloria and I have found the Chosen Few and I think that this is probably better than finding popularness. I have also found out a lot about dead foxes and a bit about boys. I guess this could be called an 'added bonus'.

It's funny how things turn out.

Truly
Tan

Are you
quizzically quizzable?
Check your knowledge with
a Truly Tan Quick Quiz

1 Gorgonzola cheese smells like ...

A ☐ spew

B ☐ sour milk

C ☐ the most disgusting cheese known to man

D ☐ all of the above

2 Ghosts are ...

A ☐ normal

B ☐ abnormal

C ☐ paranormal

D ☐ people in white sheets

3 Palm reading is ...

A ☐ more reliable than the Magic 8 Ball

B ☐ used by all the Great Detectives

C ☐ best done on a tropical island

D ☐ best left to experts like Rose

4 Doodad is ...

A ☐ not as smart as a fluffy slipper

B ☐ a Christmas decoration

C ☐ a sophisticated hunting dog

D ☐ a three-legged cat

5 Who is the best at quizzes?

A ☐ Tan Callahan

B ☐ Miss Dragone

C ☐ Ted Murphy

D ☐ Verity Crisp

6 Stuart the mouse has ...

A ☐ bad teeth

B ☐ bad hearing

C ☐ bad nerves

D ☐ bad manners

7 The sign on Wanda's shack says ...

A ☐ KEEP SMILING

B ☐ KEEP CALM

C ☐ KEEP YOUR HAIR ON

D ☐ KEEP OUT!

Answers

1. D
2. C
3. D
4. A
5. A
6. C
7. D

If you got seven right, you have been paying close attention and definitely have the mind of a Great Detective.

If you got more than four right, you probably could be a Great Detective if you were a bit more ... dedicated.

If you got less than three right, you should buy a Magic 8 Ball and ask for guidance.

Desperate for
Tan's next adventure?
Look out for

TRULY TAN: JINXED!

Available May 2013